Cybill Unbound

Catherine Hiller

CYBILL UNBOUND

Catherine Hiller

Heliotrope Books
NEW YORK

ISBN 978-1-956474-18-3
eBook ISBN 978-1-956474-19-0

Heliotrope Books LLC
heliotropebooks@gmail.com

"Her Last Affair" was first published in the *Antioch Review*.
"Cybill at Burning Man" was first published in *NextTribe*.
Some early chapters appeared in different form in *Cybill in Between*
  (Ravenous Romance).
Thanks to Stephanie Caciopoppo for her excellent book, *Wired for Love*.

Cover Design: Naomi Rosenblatt
Bodypaint Artist: Andy Golub
Some Kind of Love Poem: courtesy of M. G. Stephens

To Mark

Also by Catherine Hiller

Argentaybee and the Boonie, for children
Abracatabby, for children
An Old Friend from High School
17 Morton Street
California Time
Skin: Sensual Tales
The Adventures of Sid Sawyer
Just Say Yes: A Marijuana Memoir
The Feud

"Monogamy may or may not be natural to human beings, but transgression surely is."

—Esther Perel

"The erotic is the nurturer or nursemaid of all our deepest knowledge."

—Audre Lord

"More venery. More love; more closeness; more sex and romance. Bring it back, no matter what, no matter how old we are."

—Roger Angell

"If there's a book you want to read but it hasn't been written yet, then you must write it."

—Toni Morrison

Some Kind of Love Poem

From this position, love appears, or from
That angle, there it is, though completely
Unexpected, even a surprise, and
Maybe not even welcome, after all,
There are so many other things to do
Like going to the gym or making lists
Of things to do, love not being one of
Those items listed, and yet love is there,
Unexpectedly or not, love wants you
To know that it is all that you need or
Ever wanted, even when you ask it:
Is that all that love is? And the answer,
Of course, is, yes, that is all that love is
That is all love will ever be, and more.

—M.G. Stephens

CONTENTS

1. AIR HUNGER

1988

Cybill sipped the screwdriver she always requested when she flew. The alcohol steadied her nerves, and the vitamin C in the orange juice would, she hoped, protect her from strange germs. She was on a flight to Denver for business. After James left her for Janice, she'd gotten a job in the marketing department of a textbook company, and she sometimes had to travel to visit a client or go to a trade show.

She suddenly felt sad, contemplating her separation and the probable divorce to come. The marriage hadn't been that bad. She and James had always been fine in bed, even toward the end. They had three wonderful kids. They agreed about all the big things. True, they bickered often, but these casual jousts were "spirited." That's what she thought, anyway, although her best friend Johanna termed them, "grinding." Tears came to Cybill's eyes as she reminded herself that James had actually and permanently left her for that woman Janice. But maybe they were just alcohol tears. Maybe even one drink was a mistake when she felt like this—as fragile as a sparrow in a tempest.

In the row in front of her, a very good-looking man sat reading. He had longish dark hair, tanned skin, strong features and a curved mouth. She wondered what his eyes and teeth were like and what book he was avidly perusing. He hadn't looked up as Cybill stowed her suitcase in the overhead compartment, nor when she took off her leather coat and put that away as well. This surprised her. She was used to men looking at her, but she supposed she was too old for him. He looked to be about thirty.

She suddenly realized that at forty-two, she was probably too old for many men. What a dim future awaited. For the past twenty-five years, men had been the focus of her life—men and her children.

Now most men wouldn't want her, and her children didn't need her. She didn't think her job marketing textbooks was going to compensate for this.

Never mind. On this business trip, she would try to have fun. She was going to swim in the hotel pool, which went from indoors to outdoors on the roof; she had seen a picture of it on the hotel website. And she planned to see something of Denver, which she had never visited before, although James had gone there for business.

Suddenly, Cybill remembered her last time with James, a few weeks after he'd moved out. This was in the winter, during the lowest part of her life, when she felt she'd been discarded like an old tissue. Night after night, she woke up weeping in the dark. Her bedroom windows looked east, and when the alarm went off, the cantaloupe disk of the sun rose through the bare trees, growing smaller and brighter and paling to lemon—all within minutes. Sometimes she opened her eyes, saw the sun, and wept some more.

One morning, she awoke to find James in the bedroom. "What time is it?" she asked as she emerged, confused, from the gauze cocoon of sleep.

"Six-fifteen." He had taken off his olive-green duffle coat, and now he dropped it on a chair. He apparently didn't notice when it slid to the floor.

"What are you doing here?" she asked. She heard her own tone of voice: gentle, not outraged.

James heard it too. "I thought you might need to hug me," he said. He sat on the bed and began to tug off his boots.

She asked, "What about you?"

"I'm here, aren't I?" Then he reached for her.

His strong arms, his familiar dark beard, his special way

of thumbing her nipples. Her response was immediate and overwhelming. Her desire was so keen she cut short his caresses to indicate, in the way she had for decades, that she was ready.

As he took the first delicious strokes, she thought about Janice, whom she still had not met. Janice was the faceless, gorgeous Other Woman, the one he truly loved. But he still had one spare fuck for Cybill. This humiliating thought pushed her over the edge, and she gave a loud moan and shuddered deeply everywhere.

"I guess you *did* need a hug," he said shortly after. He began getting dressed. "I'd better leave before the kids wake up. I don't want to get them all confused."

Cybill asked, "What about me?"

"You'll be fine."

"So what was that? A mercy-fuck?"

James gave a grin. "You could always make me laugh!"

"Well, I'm not laughing, James. There's something cruel about you."

"To which you respond."

"Not any more," she said. "Out."

"I'm going, I'm going." He grabbed his jacket and fled.

They never did that again, although it was, she felt, a really good time. Unless you considered the consequences, which were none. Perhaps it was only in fiction that great sex and great emotion always went together.

She never told Johanna about this episode, feeling ashamed of both her acquiescence and that it had effected no change whatsoever in James. That brief fuck had been thrilling all right. But surely this was due to the "other woman" fantasy that had flavored the act.

Cybill went directly from the airport to the convention center to set up the company booth. Her exhibitor's pass was ready for her, and when she got to the booth space, she saw that the 17 boxes of books and journals had all arrived and were at her feet. There was no reason to be anxious. She had several hours to unpack the cartons and prepare the booth. The next day, a local temp would arrive at the exhibit hall to help take orders and sell books. Everything was proceeding as planned.

Yet Cybill took one deep breath after another without satisfaction. She was getting the breath-thing, which she sometimes got when she was anxious. At these times, no matter how deeply she breathed, she felt oxygen-starved. She felt a compulsion to yawn but was unable to do so. She knew from experience that the worst thing to do when she had these spells was to think about her breathing. Rather, she should distract herself, think about other things. She told herself it was only mental.

She started to unpack her company's books onto the metal shelves. She put three copies of *The Psychology of Grief* on display. She wondered if she was still grieving for James. She didn't think so. She often grieved for the death of her marriage, and sometimes raged that he had left her for Janice, but Cybill now realized—and, book in hand, her arm froze in the air—that *she never actually missed her ex*. She never wished James were by her side; she never yearned for him as a companion or a lover.

Yet until the day he moved out she had thought she loved him! Is it possible *not* to love someone although you think you do?

Although she was at the American Psychiatric Association's annual meeting, she doubted that this interesting question would be addressed, nor the related conundrum: can you think you're happy when you're not?

If so, perhaps fooling yourself isn't a bad idea.

Cybill thought of this the next morning, as she was getting ready for the day. In her hotel, she had a choice of mirrors by which to apply make-up. In the bathroom, there was a small, well-lit magnifying mirror, in which every pore looked like a crater and every facial hair, a boar's bristle. And there was the large bedroom mirror, which revealed her usual self: a slender buxom woman with high cheekbones and short, curly blond hair. If she avoided the magnifying mirror and fooled herself, surely she would be better off, more confident to tackle the day.

On the other hand, if she hadn't fooled herself in her marriage, she might have been more attuned to James's unhappiness, and perhaps he wouldn't have found consolation with Janice. Instead of assuming he was happy, perhaps she should have looked deeper, sought his sadness, cured his soul. Perhaps then the marriage would have lasted. Surely this would have been better for the children, who were miserable about the break-up—even Rain, who was away at college. She called twice a week to express her continuing bafflement that James had left their happy family.

Cybill sat down on the hotel bed and breathed in deeply. The breath-thing was back: She couldn't seem to get enough oxygen into her lungs. "Air hunger," she had heard this syndrome called, but that was too mild a description. "Air panic" was more like it. After all, you can go for days without food—but only a couple of minutes without oxygen. Now she was gulping like a fish, and still she couldn't get satisfaction. It's only mental, she reminded herself, and this served to soothe her.

She arrived at the convention center at eight-thirty, put on her badge, and entered the exhibit hall. She saw a banner proclaiming, "Denver is Zoloft Country." Maybe she should take Zoloft. Maybe that would help her breathe.

The most lavish booths at this show were those of the big pharmaceutical companies. One of them offered a virtual reality session to help people experience the extreme fatigue felt by the clinically depressed. Another was distributing handsome calculators imprinted with the name of a new drug for obsessive-compulsive disorder. A third company, which had a drug for Alzheimer's, offered people the chance to see how they would look in twenty years. A photo was taken, adjusted digitally, and returned in a few minutes. She made a note to stop in at that booth later in the day to see what the future would do to her face.

The temp, a perky woman of thirty, was waiting for her at the company booth. Her name was Sue Ann, and she was quick to inform her that she was really an actress. Cybill explained how it would be quiet at first because most people would be at scientific sessions. At the 10:30 coffee break, they'd get some floor traffic, and at lunchtime they would be busy. Cybill would come back at the booth when it got crowded, but for most of the day, she'd be out on the floor talking to people.

She packed her canvas bag with catalogues, price lists, and order forms. She put in a few of their best-selling books. Then she walked to the 100 aisle.

It was a good time to go booth hopping, as there were few registrants on the floor, and the exhibitors were eager to talk. All she had to do was hesitate in front of a booth and someone would call out, "Yes, can I help you?" Then she would explain who she worked for, offer a catalogue, make conversation, learn about their company, chat. Still, she was nervous approaching each new booth, which was curious. After all, it wasn't so hard to say brightly, "Good morning, I'm with Academy Publishing."

After every conversation, she scribbled notes onto a legal pad. Upon her return, she was supposed to present a report to her boss. She had spoken to reps from only five companies, out of 60, when she saw it was 10:35, and she hurried back to her booth to help Sue Ann. For half an hour, it was busy, then Cybill went back to aisle 100.

By five o'clock, her voice and feet and face were tired. She was all smiled-out. She could feel a headache building just between her brows. She was approaching the booth that would show you what the years would do to your face, so she joined the short line to have her picture taken. She hoped she'd look wise and contented. Surely in twenty years she'd be sagacious and at peace. But, she reflected, at twenty she expected to be knowing and happy by forty—which she was not.

She filled out a brief questionnaire, and then it was her turn to get photographed. She smothered the urge to raise her chin and give her usual smile. Something more restrained than a grin seemed in order. She faced the photographer, a man of her age with a ponytail, and did absolutely nothing with her face. Wise people didn't bare their teeth for the camera.

There was a flash, and the photographer said, "Thank you. Please come back in ten minutes."

Poor guy. In his youth, perhaps he'd wanted to be an art

photographer. Now he took hundreds of pictures a day at conventions. Then Cybill remembered that when she was young, she had wanted to be a college professor. Now she was just another marketing professional.

She spoke to two more exhibitors then came back to collect her photograph. A young woman wearing a nurse-like outfit handed her a small beige envelope. Cybill went to the restaurant area nearby, sat down at a round table and stared at the envelope. She wondered who she would see. She hoped that she'd go smiling through the years to meet her future self. When she got home, she could show Jesse and Daniel what she'd look like when they were all grown and she was grandma to their children. She could show her mother, who was taking care of the boys now, and they would have a fond smile over the picture. She slid the photograph out of the envelope and saw . . .

Herself. Cybill. Tense, unsmiling, anxious. Creases had been added to her forehead and the corners of her mouth. Her hair had been whitened all around her temples. There was a blur of extra flesh at her jaw-line, and the mole on her chin had been enlarged.

At the sight of this unhappy-looking older woman who looked just like her, Cybill's breath ran short again. If *this* was the future . . .

She would dye her hair. She would take Botox injections so she couldn't frown and get vertical lines between her eyebrows. She would get a face-lift, as her mother had recently done, to good results.

She would need to make a lot more money than she now earned to prevent herself from looking like the woman in the photo. Even now, it took more and more effort to look good. In fact, *not looking ugly* was the major principle of her beauty routine. It was more important to inspect her chin and tweeze any hairs than to apply cinnamon lipstick. She had to smooth cream into the lines on her cheeks and pat concealer on the shadows under her eyes. She had to throw a color rinse on her hair every few weeks to cover the gray strays, and she had to put Retin-A on her throat at night in the desperate hope of firming her neck. It was a losing battle against time's depredations, and even if she had cosmetic surgery, there was always going to be something to indicate her age: the spider veins behind her knees, the cords on the back of her hands.

The next afternoon, she stopped by the Excelsior booth and spoke to a marketing executive there. Jay Tilson was a large, pink man of fifty, with thick, dark, unnatural-looking hair. Excelsior had a new drug for schizophrenia. "You know," Cybill said, "we've just published a book on schizophrenia, and the author has a chapter on your drug. He thinks it's by far the best available pharmaceutical. Here, take a look." She pulled out the book from her canvas bag. "You might want to buy this book in bulk for your marketing purposes. We could place gift stickers in the front: 'Compliments of Excelsior.'"

"Let me see," said Jay Tilson, reaching for the book.

"Page eighty-five," Cybill said. She watched him turning pages.

"That's not a bad idea," he said after a while. "Not a bad idea at all. Let me   present it to my people when I get back. Thanks so much for stopping by." He held up the book. "Can I buy one of these?"

"You don't have to do that," Cybill sang. "Just keep it as a complimentary copy."

"If we bought the book in bulk, what would the pricing be? Say, on a thousand copies?"

"I'll have to check, of course, but I think we could go down to twenty apiece."

He nodded as if this was perfectly reasonable.

Her boss would be thrilled if they made the sale. All in all, the trip had been a success. And yet, when she got back to the booth, she was very short of breath. The air she drew in didn't seem adequate. She tried to ignore her shortness of breath. In an attempt to distract herself, she thought about a smooth, calm lake.

It didn't work. Her breathing was less and less . . . satisfying. She sat on the stool behind the high table at her booth and slumped over so that her head was lower than her knees.

God, this was awful—the worst air hunger she had ever

experienced. She breathed as steadily and deeply as possible, but it didn't feel right and she didn't feel good.

She felt indignant that she was getting air hunger now, when things were going well. She couldn't understand it. She thought of the photograph she had torn up: the anxious old lady who awaited her down the years. Was it possible to *be* anxious even if you didn't feel it?

With her head still below her knees, she looked at her watch. It was five o'clock —seven o'clock in Westchester—time to call the kids. Lately they seemed a little better about the break-up, although Daniel sometimes still said, "I wish Daddy lived with us like before."

Now Cybill tried short rapid breaths to increase her oxygen intake, but this didn't help either. She slowly raised her head until she was sitting upright. She stared ahead to steady herself. She found she was facing a banner: "Welcome to Denver, the Mile-High City."

If Denver was a mile high, then its elevation was 5,280 feet. Suddenly, she found herself smiling. Because of the altitude, oxygen really *was* thinner in Denver. She told herself that it was only physical.

Somehow, this served to soothe her.

In her mind, her friend Johanna said, "You're such a Pollyanna! Everything consoles you! Whether air hunger's mental or physical—you feel comforted either way."

"It's how I cope," she told Johanna, mentally.

She slowly stood up. She was swaying on her feet. She didn't start to walk until the dizziness went away. Then, unsteadily, she walked down the aisle toward the pay phones. She took a terrycloth headband from a pharmaceutical booth. The headband was emblazoned with the name of a drug—and the word "smile." Maybe she would give it to Johanna—an ironic little present. Then she snagged a second headband for herself.

2. ROGUE

1989

When Cybill was ready to start dating again, she learned that many things had changed since the last time she'd been single, twenty years earlier. Now, people were frightened to flirt, lest it be seen as harassment. Now, attractive men and women routinely met on the internet. Now, women were allowed to ask men out. Now, they often paid for half the date.

But the biggest difference was the change in the sexual climate, which was at once more temperate and more tempestuous than when she'd last been single. AIDS had put a damper on the notion of free love, which she had found so appealing in her hippie youth. Now, condoms were mandatory—unless a couple was "fluid bonded." This meant that they took the AIDS test together, used condoms, remained faithful, then took another test six months later. Only at that point could they have sex without "barrier protection."

As for Cybill, she scarcely knew what a condom looked like. When she'd last been single, she'd been on the pill, and during her marriage, she'd used a diaphragm. Now she read that condoms were available in colors, styles, flavors. She read that there was a rise in s & m—by which the writers did not mean Sales & Marketing. She read that the liberated woman had a store of lubricant, massage oil, condoms, and vibrators.

Cybill didn't have any of these things. (She couldn't imagine explaining such items to her children.) She didn't know how a cock ring worked. She didn't know why a woman would use ben-weh balls. She didn't know the names of the latest passion drugs. She had considered herself sexually adventurous as a young woman, before meeting her husband, James (the Perfidious). Would she now be seen as dull because she had no piercings or tattoos? Well, maybe not dull — just naïve. And, after all, some men like that. If you're a woman, competence — never mind expertise — isn't nearly as important, especially in the sexual arena. If you're a woman, it's quite all right to be a bumbling beginner. When she met Mel McCabe, she felt like she was from Kansas. Feeling this naive at her age was a turn-on in itself.

Her company had a booth at a medical meeting in Miami, and she was there, as in Denver, to make industry contacts, take orders for textbooks and gather competitive literature. During exhibit hall lulls while the registrants were in sessions, she became friendly with the people at the next booth, Bob Murchison and his assistant, Leora Nevins, of Phoenix Pharmaceuticals. They made plans to go to a Latin club in South Beach that night.

They met in the hotel lobby. As they got into a cab, they were joined by a fourth person, a scientist who worked as a consultant for Bob. The new guy piled in for the ride and sat in the front, so it wasn't until they had arrived at the club and gotten out of the cab that Cybill got a good look at him.

Mel McCabe was tall and lean, perhaps forty, with rimless glasses and a cloud of curly, shoulder-length hair. As they stood on the sidewalk, it came to her that she could fall in love with him. Then she chided herself — that was crazy. She hadn't even spoken to him yet.

Having thought "love" for even a second made her shy, so she said very little when they got to their table. The music was so loud no one could talk anyway.

After a while, Mel asked her to dance. She wondered if he felt sorry for her. But that couldn't be. He couldn't know he'd inspired the word "love." Maybe it wasn't only pity that made him want to dance with her, for she saw him sneak a glance at her breasts, which were on display in a tight beige tank top, over one of the special brassieres she always wore. Her left breast was a cup size smaller than her right breast, so she got bras in the larger size and sewed padding into the left cup. Back before James, her unequal breasts had always made her self-conscious when she was naked, although some men didn't notice.

She followed Mel downstairs to the crowded dance floor. He danced like a free-spirit, all flowing arms and hair and rolling hips. Other dancers pushed them together, and she felt Mel's heat, his sweat. The band played one irresistible dance song after another, and they just kept dancing. After a while, Bob and Leora came by to say they leaving, and Mel said, without consulting Cybill, "We're staying." After they left, she gave Mel's waist a little squeeze, and he said in her ear, "God, you are *hot*."

"It's the music," she shouted back, but she wanted to say, "Because I'm with you." She felt reckless, feckless, gorgeous. Here she was, a woman in her prime, in a strange city, with a new man. If only James could see her now! James and his horrible Janice!

When the band finally took a break, Mel said, "I've got some pot in my hotel room."

"Let's go," Cybill said, surprising herself at her eager response. He laughed, which made her laugh, too. And this made her wonder: why do we laugh so much with a new partner? Perhaps it's sudden complicity—that thrilling superiority we feel to everyone else in the world. Perhaps it's a general lowering of restraint. When we laugh, as when we come, we are out of control.

They smoked on the balcony of his hotel room, watching the moon's pale highway on the water. "Business travel," she murmured.

He took a hit, held in the smoke, then said on the exhale, "Hey, Cybill." With the tips of his fingers, he traced a filigree on her left wrist. "I think you should know. I have a girlfriend."

"That's fine." Mel lived in Boston, after all, and Cybill lived near New York City. She didn't want a long-distance romance. After the pain of James's defection, all she wanted now was some fun, a little distraction, nothing heavy. Or so she told herself. It had been more than a year since she'd been with a man, and she would have agreed to almost any terms or conditions. She croaked, "Girlfriend no problem."

They grinned at each other as if in cahoots.

Mel said, "So you're okay with some limits? In bed?"

"Sure. Limits are *great*."

"*Cool*. How's that?"

Less danger, less risk—but she just said. "I've always loved heavy petting."

"Oh, baby," said Mel. He led her inside to the bed.

He kissed her so intensely that her head was pushed off the side of the bed and her throat was all exposed. He put his mouth down to her chest, and burrowed down beneath her shirt. He began to lick her nipple.

When he took off her shirt and bra, his mouth widened in happy amazement. "Your breasts are two different sizes! That is *so* cool!"

"My ex didn't notice until after we were married."

Mel said, "I notice everything."

For the next several hours, they kissed and caressed and twisted and rubbed and sucked and nibbled each other. At one point, he said, "Play with my nipples," and she was glad, she would never have thought of this, and he got very excited, especially when she tugged. They were deeply and multiply satisfied by the time Cybill left his room at five in the morning to go to hers.

And they hadn't needed barrier protection.

She had a seven o'clock industry breakfast, and he had a seven-thirty scientific session. Oddly, she wasn't tired all day. She was totally invigorated because she knew that she might turn the corner and bump into him.

At four, just before he had to leave for his plane, they walked to the parking garage to say goodbye. (Hotel check-out time was eleven, so they couldn't go up to a room.) They kissed and grasped and swayed between a beige Explorer and a black Solera. Cybill ran her hands through his head of fine curls one more time. She almost never got to Boston, and he almost never got to New York. He cupped her behind in its corporate skirt. She let her hands drift down to his chest, and he sighed and pressed her breasts.

She became hot and weak. She could barely walk beside him to the hotel lobby, where he left on the airport shuttle bus.

The next day, back at the office, it didn't take her long to discover an interesting scientific meeting in Boston the following month. She stepped into her boss's office and said how useful it would be if Cybill could attend the conference for a couple of days. Then at night she could rendezvous with her lover. But since they weren't actually making love, was Mel actually her lover?

The phone rang, interrupting these pleasant musings. It was Cybill's boss, congratulating her on finding out about the Boston meeting and telling her to make travel arrangements.

Cybill called Mel and counted the days until Boston.

When she opened her hotel room door to let Mel in, there he was—tall and grinning—shorn! He had cut his hair: his curls were short and Grecian.

"Wow," she said.

"You like it?"

"Give me a moment to mourn your lost hippie locks."

"A moment of silence," said Mel, closing the door behind him.

They bowed their heads. Then she said, "Actually, it's a good cut. Very stylish. It makes you look even taller."

He dropped his backpack to the floor.

Cybill said, "I thought you couldn't stay the night because of Gina." Gina was his girlfriend. In the weeks since they'd met, she'd kept thinking of Mel, and she no longer felt totally nonchalant about Gina.

"I can't stay the night."

"You brought books?" Cybill joked.

"I brought some of my photographs. And also some sex toys." He drew her into his arms, and she felt hot with longing, cold with fear. They kissed deeply and lingeringly, and she felt herself getting swollen.

It didn't make sense that the chance of danger should be arousing. People procreating are defenseless: you'd think that safety would be needed for arousal to take place. This was not, apparently, the case.

When they had stopped kissing and were catching their breath she asked, "What did you bring?"

Mel unzipped his backpack and brought out a black rubber paddle. It was about the size of the bats children use to hit a ball on an elastic string. One side of the paddle was covered with soft black fur.

She asked, "Why the fur?"

"Because it feels good." He pulled her sweater off over her head. Then he took her to the bed and pushed her down flat, so her face was in the pillow. He ran the fur side of the paddle down her back. "See?"

"It is nice."

Then he lifted up her skirt and pulled off her underpants, right down and over her feet. Now she was wearing only a skirt and a bra. He lifted her skirt and brought the rubber side of the paddle down upon on her bare behind. Slap, slap, slap!

"You can*not* leave a mark!" she cried. What if her children came across a bruise on her body?

"No marks. Just a rosy glow."

"Please be careful."

"Don't worry. I'm good at this." He hit her lightly with the paddle a few times. "This is cool."

She sighed.

He said, "We have to have a code. If you want me to stop, you'll say. . . what?"

"How about 'stop'?"

"That's no good. It's a common turn-on to say 'stop' and be overcome. So we have to have a stop word that isn't 'stop.' Like 'red.'"

"'Red's fine," she said impatiently.

"I'll use 'red' too," he said, and she realized that she would get to use the paddle —or something—on him. This idea excited her. Mel was bringing out aspects of herself she never knew she had.

He caressed her buttocks now with the fur side of the paddle. "You're wonderful," he said—then brought the rubber side down on her.

Whap! It was a shock and a tingle, not painful—but scary. Perhaps that was why it was thickly erotic. He hit her several times, erratically, then asked her lovingly, "How are you, sweetie?" He touched her to find out.

That did it. As she was moaning and riding the waves, she heard herself say, "I am yours." Then she turned over and dozed for a while.

She woke up to the languid caress of something on her back. It wasn't his hand, and it wasn't the paddle. It was lighter, dryer, somehow multiple. He flicked whatever it was on her buttocks to make a quick zing. "You have the most wonderful ass," he told her. "It's just so exciting." Zing, zing!

"What do you have there?" she asked, rolling over and sitting up.

"This is my flogger," said Mel.

She held out her hand and he gave it to her by the rawhide handle, from which dangled a bouquet of fringes, maybe a foot long.

"I could stroke you with this," she said thoughtfully. She shimmied the tails over his chest. "Or I could strike you." She brought the thing down on the tops of his thighs. He moaned.

She improvised like this for some time, talking softly, flicking the thing on him, touching him, making him crazy.

Making him scream.

Then she got a towel and wiped them both dry.

"That was a first for me," she said conversationally.

"That's hard to believe. How did you learn how to top?"

"From years of bottoming. Mainly in my mind."

"Cool."

"What's amazing is how similar they feel."

"The flogger and the paddle?" Mel asked.

"No." she pushed her hand into his mouth. "Topping and bottoming."

❁ ❁ ❁

Once she was home, Cybill wondered if perversion inevitably escalated. Would she and Mel have to go further and further to

keep it hot and new? What would they do next? She thought
about Mel too much: while driving, while shopping, while
making dinner, while taking a shower. She'd wake up in the
middle of the night from dreams of Mel only to find myself alone
and aroused. She'd creep to the bathroom and look at her face
in the mirror. Bad girl! Dreaming of another woman's man. She
felt guilty. She felt great. She felt helpless, driven by desire. The
thought excited her anew: to be feeling all this at her age!

She knew lust was no excuse at all—but it was an explanation.

When David Shalom, one of her married cousins, had run off
with their Swedish au pair, Uncle Moses had shrugged and said,
"Jeh-jeh always wins." "Jeh-jeh" meant penis or lust.

Jeh-jeh was ruling her life, or should she say *ruining*. Jeh-jeh
was sending her to secret assignations, avid for Mel's complex
kisses and simple commands: "Don't move." "Look into my
eyes." "Pull my nipples, baby."

She wondered why he liked that so much. What she liked was
getting his instructions, whatever they were.

Finally—finally!—Mel came to New York. She knocked on
the door of his hotel room. He opened the door and took her in
his arms at once. Full frontal meltdown.

At last, she stepped away and asked, "How was your meeting?"

"It was great. I arranged it so I could see you, but it looks like
they're going to give me some business."

"See how good for you I am."

"You are, baby, you are."

Soon, they were naked on the bed, writhing, rubbing,
mouthing. He lifted his mouth from her breasts and said, "I want
to take your picture."

She shook her head.

He said, "Please."

"No." She had seen other nudes he had taken—shameless
females, beautiful pictures—and she knew he would use her
photograph the same way: to excite and seduce other women. The
better the picture, the better he would seem as a photographer
and lover.

And he *was* a good lover. He moved downward in the bed. He adored giving head, always wanted to, hallelujah!, kept saying she was delicious. She opened her legs to accommodate his mouth, and soon she was helpless and sighing. He brought one of her knees up, to spread her even wider. Then he pulled away. She assumed he was getting some sex toy and kept her eyes closed to sustain the spell he'd created.

The spell was broken when she heard a brief buzz, and she opened her eyes just in time to see the first flash. He was down at the bottom of the bed, taking pictures with a reflex camera, and he quickly took two more before she wrenched the camera away from him. "That is so wrong!" She cried. She must have put her hand on the shutter because there was another flash. (The photo, when developed, would prove to be a close up of his elbow and the sheet.) Then the camera began groaning and clicking as the camera rewound the film. "Convenient," she said. "What else is on the roll?" He said, "Why do you ask?"

"I want the roll."

"Oh, Cybill, you don't mean that."

"Yes, I do."

Mel opened the camera, took out the exposed film, and fumbled around in his camera bag for the protective plastic canister. "Look, " he said, "I just want those photos for myself. I promise I won't show them to anyone."

"You don't have to promise because I'm going to keep them."

He was physically stronger than she was, but she had the advantage, because sneaking shots of her yoni had made him very hard.

"No pay, no play," she said. Shaking his head dolefully, Mel handed her the canister, which she stashed inside an inner pocket of her handbag. Then he held out his arms, and it was achingly sweet just to touch him. How outrageous he was — taking advantage of her like that.

They rolled upon the bed. "How are you?" he asked, sliding his fingers into her. He found his answer, smiled and said, "Oh, my!"

And that was all it took.

Ah, but she was premature. Over the next half hour Mel twisted her around, this way and that, rubbing against her and showing no signs of coming himself. After a while, he said, "Pull on my nipples, baby," so she did. When she brought her hands down to cup his balls, he said, "Don't stop touching my nipples," so she brought her mouth to his chest and began sucking. It was a wonderful feeling, and Mel was now breathing hard. She got into a rhythm, sucking first one nipple then the other. She felt both excited and at peace, and Mel was pulling his cock hard and gasping. Then he spurted and was still. "Oh, my sweetie," he said. "I love you."

Her eyes filled with tears.

He stroked her hair and asked, "What are you feeling?"

"Overwhelmed. Terrified."

"It's okay, sweetie."

"Sweetie" had become the most exciting and beautiful word in the English language.

Mel said, "It's cool."

"Maybe not," Cybill said. Hearing of his love had been like gentle rain on her heart, and now it was opening, blossoming. But they lived in different cities. And he had a girlfriend named Gina. And maybe he said "I love you" all the time.

"Talk to me," said Mel.

She didn't know what she could say. She took his hand and rested it comfortingly on herself.

He said, "You're amazing."

In the middle of the night, she got up and took her handbag to the bathroom. She checked that the canister of film was still there. She took it out of the compartment in her handbag and absently gave it a shake. She heard a faint rasp, as if from a tail of unexposed film. She opened the canister and found that this was true. When he'd been fumbling in his camera-case, Mel had replaced the shots of her with some new film that had nothing on it. Somehow, she was not surprised.

By the open bathroom door, she had enough light to see where his camera case was, and she brought it into the bathroom. She found the roll of exposed film and replaced it with the new film he had given her. She put the exposed film into her handbag, which she put into the bottom drawer of the dresser. Mel was still asleep when she crept into bed.

His treachery and her triumph made her very excited, and she had to wake him up. He obliged her at his pace. He sucked her a while then made her wait while he thrust himself into her mouth. He said, "I love doing anything I want with you." He brought his mouth down again.

"Almost anything," she reminded him, for they still hadn't fucked.

"Somehow, I don't feel deprived," Mel murmured. "Do you?"

"De*praved*," she corrected.

On her way home from work the next day, she dropped off the roll of film at the drugstore.

Mel called her at work first thing Monday morning and said, "You switched the film on me!"

"You switched the film on me first."

"I can't believe you did that. You vixen!"

"I can't really talk now."

"Then listen. You didn't take the film in to be developed, did you?"

"Of course I did."

"Cybill! That's dangerous!"

"It just goes out to some lab, Mel. What's the big deal?"

"I wish you hadn't done this."

"You knew I didn't want pictures taken of me. Not like that! You violated my trust!"

"Listen, Cybill, you could get in trouble. There's some heavy stuff on that roll."

"Really? I thought film developing was all automatic."

"Not entirely. Sometimes there's a jam and they have to cut the strips manually. And then if they see explicit photographs, they might say it's pornography and refuse to send it back. Or they might circulate the pictures on the internet. You never know."

"Jesus!"

"I have a special lab I use where I trust the people."

"Well, I trust the anonymous lab," Cybill said, but she began to get nervous.

"It's probably cool," said Mel, "but call me when you get the pictures back."

"Sure."

"And, remember. I love you."

She was holding the phone hard against her ear while the office around her dissolved. This was how he really made her nuts: with those three little words, with that shattering phrase.

She herself had said "I love you" to only one man, James.

Of course, it might be different for Mel, who had never been married. He was a career adventurer, an explorer. He had many playmates and a bag of toys. He had that New Age, Loving More mentality.

Still, maybe Mel thought she was his soul-mate, his true love, his fate.

Sometimes she thought Mel was hers.

"How can you possibly say that?" demanded Johanna. "You haven't spent twenty-four hours total together."

"We're just so alike emotionally. We're very intense and very, uh, fucked up. We make each other crazy."

"You're drawn to him because he's fucked up?"

"Isn't *that* fucked!"

Now she said into the telephone mouthpiece to Mel, "*Don't* say 'I love you.'"

"Why not?"

"Just don't." She saw her world splitting open so she could love Mel fully in return. She imagined quitting her job, selling her house, packing Daniel and Jesse to live with James and Janice, and moving up to Boston, near Rain at college, so she could live with Mel.

"But I do love you," Mel said. "Don't you believe me?"

"Love can mean many things," she temporized. "How many women have you said 'I love you' to?"

Mel was silent for a while. "In my life?"

"Yes."

"I don't know," said Mel. "Maybe twenty-five."

She gave an astonished cry. Then she began to laugh—with relief, she told herself.

"What?" asked Mel.

"My boss wants to see me," she lied. "I have to go."

Twenty-five! So she didn't have to quit her job and all that, after all! All day she would think "twenty-five" and start to giggle.

She also congratulated herself. She was far less keen on him now (she told herself every five minutes) than she had been before "twenty-five." Perhaps this meant she had grown up. In the past, before James, a man's treating her casually would have made her more obsessed. And she wasn't obsessed. Not really.

She picked up the photographs that evening and locked the door of her bedroom before opening the yellow film processing bag.

The first few shots were of a naked, sinewy woman with very small breasts and a ring in her navel. No doubt this was Gina, the girlfriend, who was thirty-three. She was posing outdoors, on a deck, near some plants. The next shots were of Mel, naked, lolling in a chair. His cock was glistening, and its head looked very big. He held it lightly with his fingers. Gina was with him in the next few pictures—Mel must have used a self-timer. Then came some pictures of Mel tied up on the bed, and Cybill looked at these with interest. He was fully erect. It would be great to have him tied and helpless, she would have such fun . . .

By contrast, the shots of herself were almost arty. The simplicity of the photographs made them semi-abstract, and because of the angle, you couldn't see her face, thank God. So much for the internet threat.

She turned back to the pictures of Mel tied and spread-eagled.

She wondered whether sadomasochism was a retreat from feeling and whether role-playing somehow diminished emotion. Perhaps—on the contrary—kinky sex made lovers even closer, as they broke taboos together.

She called Mel at his office, for she knew he worked late. "I got the pictures back," she said. "No problem."

"Cool. And?"

"I love the ones of you tied up."

"Wait a minute," he said. "Let me shut the door to my office." He returned to the phone.

She asked, "Are you all safe and private?"

"Uh-huh."

"Are you touching yourself?"

"Uh-huh."

"Will you bring some leg and arm restraints next time we meet?"

"Yes."

"And some rope. So I can tie you up."

"Yes. Baby."

"And then I'll have fun with you," she said. "You'll be at my mercy."

He panted and said, hoarsely, "God, I love you."

Twenty-five! She said, "I'm going to punish you."

"Tell me."

"Well, now I've got the paddle, and I'm kind of hitting you randomly here and there." She described various things, then said, "Now I'm getting rather bored, so I'm switching to the flogger. I'm running it up and down your legs, gently, gently."

She continued, getting rougher, for a while.

Then she said, "And now I'm holding a vibrator. I'm turning it on, and it's got a soft purr. And first, I'm running it on your chest to stimulate your left nipple. Then your right nipple. And now I'm removing it, Mel, and you don't know what I'm going to do next. What I'm going to do next is . . . to put the vibrator hard on the base of your balls."

"Ahhhhh!" It was a gasp torn from his center. "Ahhh! Ah." Then Mel was silent.

"You okay?" she asked.

"You're incredible," he said. "That was great."

Cybill marveled at this new side of herself that sometimes

emerged in their fluidly changing dominant/submissive dynamic. With Mel she could be anything at all—a slave, a dominatrix, a patient on the table, a libidinous masseuse. She could even give telephone sex.

Two weeks later, Mel was back in New York for the weekend. As always, she arrived at Mel's hotel room on a tide of desire.

Mel said, "I have a surprise for you."

"Another sex toy?"

"You'll see."

She put her tongue in his ear. He dug his fingers into her buttocks.

She unbuttoned his shirt and pushed it aside. And that's when she saw, on his nearly hairless chest, a gold stud through his right nipple.

Mutilation! A nipple! She felt a wave of . . . she couldn't say exactly what. Some mixture of repulsion and arousal. She was appalled and excited at once.

"You can touch it," said Mel.

"Maybe I don't want to."

"Sure you do. Sweetie. Do it for me."

These words proved irresistible. She brought her hand to his chest and felt the two nubs of metal in the sensitive flesh of the nipple-tip.

Mel closed his eyes.

"Does it really feel good?" She asked, caressing him lightly.

"Oh, yeah. Sweetie."

Next thing, he'd be saying he loved her again, and she couldn't bear that.

But why should she take him seriously? A man who'd had his nipple pierced—a man of forty who kept saying, "Cool." A man who'd said "I love you" to twenty-five women.

She fondled the stud, and he moaned.

She said, "This *is* fun to fool with."

He was breathing hard.

She said, "This makes *you* a sex-toy."

She yanked the stud lightly.

Mel was totally into it.

❊ ❊ ❊

They demanded nothing of each other—only ecstasy. Because of the kink factor, and because they saw each other only rarely, their passion rose ever higher. They had laughed and cried and come together—sometimes all at once. Much of their sex was laced with the possibility of danger, physical and emotional. He would gaze into her eyes and say, "I love you, Cybill. Sweetie." The intensity of their connection left her hollow later. After their encounters, it took her days to recover.

Johanna was highly dubious about Mel. "I don't know, Cybill . . . "

"What?"

"He just doesn't sound very nice. He sounds like an egotistical sex freak."

"Well, he's not. It's true he doesn't have a wife and kids, but he has friends, a good job, a busy life."

"Yeah, going to sex workshops every weekend."

"Not *every* weekend. And I'm the happy beneficiary. He went to a workshop on cunnilingus, and I asked if they showed videos, and he said no, they used live models."

"Gross!"

"Well, he's pretty out there. I guess sex is his hobby. Maybe it's mine as well. He's making me as perverse as he is!"

Silence from Johanna. Since Johanna had once more broken off with her boyfriend, Josh, apparently she did not appreciate hearing about sexual joy. Cybill thought of something she'd enjoy hearing. "Frankly, the worst thing about Mel is his New Age nonsense."

Johanna perked up. "How do you mean?"

"He's into every sort of silliness. Past lives, astrology, crystals."

"I thought you said he was a scientist."

"He is! That's what's so weird. He has these idiotic beliefs. And after these sex or spiritual workshops, he claims he's gone through this vast transformation. But I never see any change at all! Not that I *want* him to change."

"He sounds like a classic Peter Pan. He'll never grow up."

"You may be right."

            ✿ ✿ ✿

"I want you to do me a favor," Mel said on the phone to her at work later that day. They were going to meet in Atlanta, three weeks later, at a medical convention.

"What's that?" Cybill asked, uncrossing her legs and swiveling her chair to the window, where if she spoke softly, she had a modicum of privacy. She could feel sweat breaking out over her ears and a flush covering her face. It thrilled her to realize that in middle age (a term she had finally accepted), she was having the hottest affair of her life. When she saw his email name in her inbox or heard his voice on the phone, she got an instant erotic reaction. Since at her request he communicated with her only at work, she would often, as now, find herself in full arousal in the middle of a busy office. Looking down, she saw the shape of her hardened nipples poking through the fabric of her bra and silk sweater.

"Angel-baby," said Mel. "Don't shave your armpits until we meet. Then I can do it for you."

She gave a splutter of laughter and asked, "Why would you want to do that?"

Mel said, "You'll see."

She whispered into the phone, "You want me to grow my armpit hair just so you can do this?"

"Trust me. You'll like it, too. Have I ever suggested anything you haven't liked?"

He had a point.

The next morning, her shower was thirty seconds shorter than usual. She was glad it was winter, so satisfying Mel's strange demand wouldn't be visible to all and sundry. She had always thought armpit hair was sexy because it had the texture of pubic hair. A woman's hairy armpits were like two ancillary pussies. Surely the reason women shaved was so they wouldn't drive men crazy. But Mel didn't want to just *see* her armpit hair: he wanted to shave it. The man was unfathomable.

From then on, every morning after her shower, she would hold the magnifying mirror to her armpits. She was always disappointed. Her blondish/brownish hair was scanty and short. Ten days into the experiment, it was scarcely visible. Well, she was doing her best for her lover, her twisted paramour. She remembered how they had once sat at a café in Boston, holding hands and locking eyes, unable to eat or drink they were so charged with sex and emotion. Her longing for Mel grew to such a pitch that it was hard to concentrate on anything else. Lost in memory and fantasy, she was abstracted, inefficient, absent. She knew she should probably end this affair, which was stopping her from wanting to meet other men — but how many people can deny themselves ecstasy?

Not *this* angel-baby, she thought.

"Are you growing your hair for me, sweetie?" Mel asked the following week. She enjoyed not answering his question. He would find out for himself in three days. By now, her axillary hair, while hardly impressive, was definitely visible, even from a little distance.

As neither she nor Mel had friends or family in Atlanta, they fell upon each other at the airport. After their lengthy embrace, she pulled her rollaway valise down the corridor at a wobble.

"Having trouble with that suitcase?" he asked smugly.

"Not at all!"

When they were driving down the highway in his rental car, she put something in his right hand, something from the day before she had placed in her pocket that morning.

"What's this?"

"My panties."

He brought them to his nose at once. He took a sniff, and the car began veering right, toward the guardrail . . .

"Careful!" she cried, and he corrected the drift. She said, "That was a close shave!"

He sniffed her panties again.

Cybill said, "Give them back if they're making you crazy!"

"But you *want* to make me crazy! That's why you did this!"

"Yes, but I don't want to get us killed."

In fact, and this was the scariest part of their affair, she had occasionally thought about their dying during an encounter: death in each other's arms, with each of them   happier than they'd ever been. She really *should* end this affair, for her own sanity. Somehow, and possibly without meaning to, Mel was pushing her toward the abyss.

When they got to his hotel room, they had hello sex just so they could have a normal conversation afterwards. A normal naked conversation. She asked about his work, he asked about hers. She asked about Gina, he asked about her children. He moved his hand up her side and into her armpit. He gave a happy cry: "Ooh! Angel-baby! Thank you, I love you." He ran his fingers up and down the stubble before leaving the bed for his toy-bag. He took out a steel bowl, shaving cream, a shaving brush, and a razor. He went to the bathroom, and she heard him filling the bowl with water.

She said, "We don't have to shower. . .?"

"Oh, no," he called. "You just stay comfortable." He took a candle out of his toy bag and lit it. Then he returned to the bed with a towel and his tools. She lifted her right arm and rested her hand on the pillow. He stroked and tickled her armpit before applying the shaving cream. Then he brought the razor to her. He used very short strokes and kept dipping the razor into the warm water to rinse off the shaving cream.

Cybill asked herself: was this exciting? Well, actually . . . *yes*. Watching Mel frowning and scraping in concentration, having this particular naked lover grooming her body like a servant was pure heaven. And in between strokes of the razor, he was also touching her here and there — wherever he wanted. If he was her servant, he was certainly taking liberties. Never before had she been groomed and petted at once. A little sigh escaped her.

"You see," Mel said.

In a little while, he dried off the armpit with a towel. Then he kissed and sucked the fresh skin.

"Only one more to go," she said dolefully. Even with his tools and his lingering, the first armpit hadn't taken more than a few minutes.

"You're making me so happy," said Mel, and she noticed he had a chubby.

She put her left hand up behind her head, and he began working on her left armpit. "Oh my God!" she said. "I just got this flash from my childhood!"

"About armpits?"

"Uh-huh."

"Tell me, sweetie. Tell me everything." He was scraping and fondling her as before, and she had to swallow to talk normally.

"Well, my mother, Rochelle, was a very beautiful woman. She still is, even now in her seventies."

"I can believe that," said Mel. He ran his fingers over her face.

"Anyway, between her first two marriages, my beautiful mother posed for an artist who painted her, fully clothed, in a green sleeveless blouse. She had her left hand in back of her head, like mine is now. It was a very good likeness. I don't know if she shaved or not, but the artist put all this black hair in her armpit. Perhaps for that reason, she never hung the painting on a wall. It stayed in some corner of the basement. My stepfather hated the picture, and one day, in deference to him, my mother put it out with the trash. I noticed it against the garbage cans as I left for school. When I came back from school at lunchtime, I saw a garbage truck going down the street. And carefully attached to a high place on the back of the truck—for safekeeping— there was that picture of my mother, black armpit and all! I was horribly embarrassed to have her up on that truck, with that hairy armpit exposed! What would the neighbors say?"

Mel said, "They were probably saying, 'Yum, yum!' Just a little more here. . ." And he gave her another stroke or two with the razor. "There. We're done."

"That was lovely," she said as he dried her off. "I feel so cared for."

"I love to care for you, give you what you need." And he lowered his head and moved down on her.

After a minute or so, she said, "Maybe you could turn around and put it in my mouth. Hard." she muttered urgently, "Like, against the back of my throat."

"Angel-baby," said Mel. "I could do that—but you have to say, 'please.'"

"*Bitte*," she said in German, without knowing why.

And because she was such a good girl, he gave her just what she wanted.

Afterwards, he moved around in the bed to hold her in his arms and caress her smooth armpits for a few minutes. Then he pulled away from her. She asked anxiously, "Where are you going?"

"Just to the bathroom." And he walked a few feet away and into the bathroom. He peed into the toilet with the door open.

"I could never do that," she observed.

"What?" he called over the splashing.

"Pee with you watching."

He shook himself off and flushed the toilet. "Sure you could," he said. "There's nothing to it."

"I'd get stage fright."

"You'll never know unless you try."

"Well, it doesn't interest me."

"You brought it up, so it must." Mel came back to the bed and began stroking her hair. "Go on. Give it a try."

The thing was, she *did* have to go. And she didn't want to seem like a timid old stick-in-the-mud. "Oh, all right. But don't expect much."

She walked to the toilet and sat down. He observed her from the bed.

At first, it was as she'd predicted. Nothing was happening. She couldn't let it loose while he was watching. "It's no good."

Mel walked to the sink and turned on the faucet. The water pattered into the sink.

Suddenly she felt a trickle seep out of her, and then a little more. And soon it was all going down, such relief, such release!

She closed her eyes, abandoning herself to urination. It kind of felt like she was coming.

She opened her eyes. He was tenderly smiling at her, and as the last drops splattered into the toilet bowl, he reached down and cupped her smaller breast lovingly.

Tears came to her eyes as she stared into his. No one had loved her like this—breasts, armpits, pee and all—no one. She was *his* angel-baby, and she'd follow him anywhere—Atlanta, Boston, the abyss.

She thought about how she could tell him this, without crowding him.

But before she could think of a way, the room telephone rang. Perhaps, she thought guiltily, it was one of her kids. She reached for the phone—but Mel pushed her hand away roughly, grabbed the receiver himself, and said, "Hello?"

She stared at him, astonished—then realized that they were in Mel's hotel room, not hers. And Mel was saying, "Nothing much. . . I just got in . . . I miss you, too, sweetie . . . Sure I do."

Cybill got out of bed and walked to the window, to give him some privacy. But she could still hear him talking softly. "Baby. You know I do. . . mmmmmm. . . sweetie. Angel-baby."

It was like cold water in her face.

Mel hung up the phone, and she returned to the bed.

"That was Gina," he said.

"I gathered."

He asked, "Why were you grabbing the phone?"

"I got all confused. I thought this was my room. I'm sorry."

"No harm done," said Mel. "But that was a close shave!"

She said, "In more ways than one."

Had she been crazy? Follow him anywhere? When she didn't even merit her own special endearments? Mel had probably watched Gina pee—and had held her breast, too. He had probably taken twenty-five women to the same places he had taken her. It might be a big deal for Cybill, but it was probably routine for him. She began putting on her clothes. To save time, she stuffed her bra into her bag before putting on her shirt.

He raised his body to lean on his elbow. "Hey, where are you going?"

Cybill said, "I thought *I* was your angel baby."

Mel said, "You *are* my angel baby."

"And so is Gina!"

"Sure."

"And the twenty-three others!"

"Twenty-three . . . what?"

"You've said 'I love you' to twenty-five women! That's twenty-five angel babies."

"I suppose," said Mel. "What of it?"

"I can't explain." She went to the door with her bag on her shoulder. "I have to go to my room, get some sleep."

He said, "Just let me kiss you goodnight."

He crossed the room and swiftly drew up her shirt. With the other hand, he held her arm forcibly up in the air. Then he kissed her pampered armpit deeply, as no one had before, and as no one would again.

3. JEW GIRL

1992

On their first date, Quinn informed Cybill that he was of Norwegian and Irish descent. They had met in a bookstore a few days earlier, and now they were in a café, awaiting their coffee.

She said, "That explains why you look like a Viking."

"What about you?" Quinn asked. "Where are your parents from?"

"I'm Jewish. My parents were born in New York, but my grandparents came from Egypt."

"So, you're Sephardic," said Quinn.

"Uh-huh." Ashkenazi Jews came from Europe; Sephardic Jews came from Spain, via the MidEast. She asked, "How do *you* know this stuff?"

His right hand touched the crown of his head, tugged his ear, and traveled down to his lap. He said, "I know a lot about the Jews."

"Really? Why?"

"Because the Jews are the smartest and most beautiful people in the world."

"We are a plucky people," she allowed.

"The best," he said passionately. "Look at how much the Jews have achieved! Out of all proportion to their numbers. Freud," he said reverently. "Marx. Einstein."

"Freud and Marx have lost some of their allure."

"Their place in history is assured," he replied.

Quinn had been a history major. He had written his senior

dissertation on Jews in America. He knew more about the *Partisan Review* crowd than she did. In fact, his knowledge and appreciation of Jews in general was much greater than her own. She didn't keep kosher. She didn't know Hebrew. She didn't belong to a temple or believe in God. Although born in New York City of Jewish parents, she wore her Jewishness lightly, like a bracelet made of straw. She considered herself Jewish merely by cultural preference (Jews worshipped learning and fought for the oppressed) and ceremonial pleasure. She liked fasting and breaking fast, lighting candles and eating matzo. But she celebrated Christmas as enthusiastically as she did Chanukah.

Although most of her Jewish friends (agnostic in their youth) now belonged to synagogues, she never felt the pull of religion, organized or otherwise. Her children had not gone to Hebrew school, and she marveled that Johanna was studying to be bat mitzvah, at age forty-eight. Cybill certainly didn't apply a Jewish litmus test to every individual she encountered, as Quinn did.

"She's one," Quinn said one night three weeks later. They were on her living room couch, watching a movie on TV. Her children were with James for the night, which presented her and Quinn with a rare and private opportunity (there were house-mates at his place). She was certainly ready for it! This was their fourth date, so surely they had earned the right to enjoy each other's bodies.

"Who's one? One what?" she asked, preoccupied with whether or not tonight would be The Night.

"Winona Ryder," Quinn replied. "She's Jewish."

"So what?"

"It explains why she's so beautiful."

Cybill giggled and said, "You're so funny on this subject."

"I just love the best people in the world. Including you. Especially you."

She blushed. It was his first declaration. "You hardly know me," she protested.

"I know what I love." He reached out, touched her nose, and said, "Tag, you're it!" Then he stroked her nose.

Cybill wondered: did she have a Jewish nose? She hoped not. Then an odd thought occurred to her. Italians like to be told they look Italian. Swedes enjoy looking Swedish. People with Cherokee or Sioux blood are happy to look like their ancestors. Only Jews are insulted to hear that they look like who they are. She asked, "Quinn, do I look Jewish?"

"Sort of. When I met you I was hoping. Your olive skin. Your voluptuous body. Your high cheekbones."

"And my nose?"

"I couldn't be sure about the nose," he said. "I mean, it's long, but it isn't curved. I love your nose." And he continued stroking it.

No one, including James, even including Mel, had ever stroked her nose before. It was curiously pleasant. She stroked Quinn's nose so he would know the feeling. Then she looked at this nose she was fondling. It was a long nose, without a curve—a nose much like her own.

He said "When I first saw you in the bookstore, I thought, 'I'll die if I don't date that woman.'"

She gave a splutter of laughter.

"What?" asked Quinn.

"Isn't that a bit extreme?"

"I'm just relating what I thought—though I didn't think 'date.'"

"Oh, you bad thing!" Cybill was delighted and amazed at her effect on him. She was not, after all, a former model or an ex-movie star: she was merely a blonde in the middle of her life.

Sexual attraction was a mystery. Why was Quinn so drawn to her? Because she was a sexy older woman? Because their noses were similar? Because she was different and exotic: Jewish?

She knew why she was drawn to him. He looked great and smelled great and was tender and kind. And now he was tugging at her shirt, so she pulled it over her head for him—glad she had bought a new lace brassiere. But he removed it at once, and, that done, he held her breasts, as if weighing them. Here we go, she thought. He's going to comment about their different sizes.

But no, he just breathed hard and said, urgently, "Cybill."

She was silent, dissolving. She let him take off all her clothes, then watched as he took off his. His body was long and white and perfect. She just said, "Oh, my!" Then she closed her eyes and opened her arms. His skin was so soft that when she touched his back, it seemed to stroke her in return.

She stopped hearing the television, stopped noticing its flicker.

She generally preferred a slow approach, but quite soon Quinn moved on top of her, and she reached down to help him get inside her. And it was *absolutely* right! Just the right size, just the right angle, just the right speed—she felt all hot and sweet. He began moving more quickly, and she wondered if he could hold out for her—but he did, oh heaven, he did!

Then he pounded away for some minutes more. Ecstatic, she internally termed these "bonus minutes." Then he surged and lay still.

They lay in happy silence for a while. She caressed his smooth arms. He stroked her hair. The television was still on, and she was hearing its sounds again. She reached around until she found the remote and turned it off.

After a few minutes, she asked, "Why were you hoping I was Jewish? I mean, besides the braininess part?"

To her surprise, he reddened.

"You're blushing!" she announced. "Goodness, what is it?" She left the couch to get them more wine. He sat up and pulled on his boxers.

"Everyone knows about Jewish women," Quinn mumbled. He touched his head, pulled his ear, returned his hand to his lap.

"What about them?" she asked, pouring wine.

"They're great in bed. They're really into it."

"They are? We are?"

"Oh, yeah. You, too, babe."

Now it was her turn to blush. Despite her times with Mel, she was sure she didn't do anything unusual in bed. She returned to the couch with the wine. He put his hand on her larger breast, and she closed her eyes. After a while she said, "I'm sure I don't do anything unusual in bed."

"Maybe not, but you really dig it."

She managed to say, "And is *that* all it takes for a woman to be a good lover?"

"That's most of it," he said, pushing her flat down upon the couch.

She marveled as she felt his penis growing hard against her stomach.

She needed a little more time to recover, so she said, "Quinn, my aunt has asked me to her annual Seder. It's this big family dinner on the first night of Passover next month. Do you want to come with me?"

He looked beatific, as if she'd just produced two tickets to the Super Bowl. "I'd *love* to!" he said. "Can I wear one of those beanie-hats?"

"Beanie-hats? Oh, you mean yarmulkes! Sure, she has extras."

"I've always wondered how they stay on."

"Men with a lot of bouncy hair—like yours—sometimes use a little bobby pin."

"A bobby pin! Then I'll be a double cross-dresser!" Quinn seemed entirely enchanted. He said, "I'm so excited! I've read about Seders and how wonderful they are."

Cybill said, "Contain your excitement. It's mostly a history lesson, confusingly told. And you can't come with me if you're going to announce how much you love Jews!"

"Especially Jewesses."

"Quinn, that is *not* an acceptable word!"

"Why not?"

"It's like 'Negress.' Or 'poetess.' It just isn't used any more."

"What a shame. It's such a lovely and exciting word. Can you feel how much I love this particular Jewess?"

"I was trying to ignore this thing poking against me," she said happily. For oddly enough, she was ready again.

As they made love a second time, she tried to hide the pleasure she was getting from Quinn's strong, Christian body.

"You can't fool me," he said with satisfaction later. "You may have kept silent, but I felt you, all right! My passionate girlfriend. My sexy little Jew girl."

A surge of after-excitement went through her. Was that what she really was? And at her great age, too! "My big butch fella," she replied. "My goy-toy."

He didn't seem to mind the appellation.

A few days later, she bought a star of David on a gold chain. The next time she saw Quinn, she wore her new necklace under her green sweater. She felt as mischievous and saucy as if she was wearing a red lace garter belt under a long black skirt. At the end of the evening, they went to his apartment, because, for a change, his house-mates were away. Quinn took off her sweater and saw her new necklace. He gave a cry of joy. Then he took the star into his mouth and kissed her neck. He twisted the chain with his finger. Again and again, he picked up the star and let it fall lightly against her collar bone. His face looked blissful and stupid and beautiful, so she closed her eyes. She looked blissful and stupid herself, she'd observed, when she was aroused.

She considered that maybe the Xandria collection of sex toys should include religious symbols.

And then she didn't have any thoughts at all for a short and happy time.

"Nice boxers," she said, when he was getting dressed again. They were silk, with narrow violet stripes against a black background.

"I got them just for you," said Quinn. "They were on sale at Macy's—only $ 9.99. Such a deal!" He said "such a deal" with a heavy Yiddish accent, and although she felt somewhat uneasy, she couldn't help laughing. Like many musicians, Quinn was very good at accents and mimicry. She watched him put ordinary jeans and an ordinary shirt over his glorious body so he could walk her to her car. Why did she feel so uncomfortable with his Yiddish accent? Maybe it was akin to how Blacks felt about the word "nigger." They used it all the time—but only Blacks had that privilege. She was about to mention her qualms to Quinn when he asked, "When can I see you again?" One of the great things about seeing Quinn was he always arranged for their next meeting before they parted, so she never had to agonize about whether she would hear from him again. In this, as in most things, he was entirely unlike Mel.

Quinn asked, "Are you free on Friday?" She watched absently as his hand went to his head and his ear then traveled down to rest by his side.

She fumbled through her bag and looked at her date-book. On Friday, she was seeing Jesse in a school play, so they agreed to meet Saturday instead.

Only after she had started the car and driven away did she realize she had never gotten to talk to him about Jewish jokes and Yiddish accents. It would not be an easy conversation.

She wondered when she'd be comfortable enough to ask him about his head-scratch/ear-tug tic. She supposed he was he suffering from some sort of obsessive/compulsive disorder, and she was curious about whether he'd been to a therapist or tried medication.

The following week, they drove into the city for a symposium on Ernest Hemingway. Six writers and critics gave short talks, and then there was a showing of a new film portrait. Quinn had read *The Old Man and the Sea* in high school; she had just re-read *A Farewell to Arms*.

They met Johanna during the intermission. Johanna was wearing a scoop-necked black sweater, and her straight brown hair was shiny and elegantly cut so it hung just a fraction of an inch above her shoulders. "So, you came, after all," Cybill said. "Where are you sitting?"

"In the back. With Josh."

"With *Josh*?" Just the day before, Johanna had told her that her on-again off-again affair with Josh was definitely over.

Johanna said, "I couldn't resist him."

"You never can," Cybill said. She wished she could do something geometric and interesting with her own hair, but curly hair is difficult to style. However it is cut and set, the next day it reverts to type.

"Aren't you going to introduce us?" asked Johanna, looking at Quinn.

"Sorry. Johanna Goldstein, meet Quinn Johnston. Quinn, you've heard me talk about my great friend Johanna."

"Many times." They shook hands.

"I've heard a bit about you, too," said Johanna.

"I wish I knew what," said Quinn. His hand moved to his head then traveled to his ear.

"You'd blush with pleasure," said Johanna. Then the lobby lights dimmed to indicate they should return to their seats.

"So, what did you think of the evening?" Cybill asked Quinn as they were walking to his car.

"It was great! Very stimulating! Interesting stuff about his masculinity."

"Yes, that was amazing." They had learned that America's most macho writer wore dresses until he was five.

Quinn said, "And what an audience!"

"How do you mean?"

"So intelligent! Such interesting questions! And such great-looking women!"

"Really?" Cybill hadn't noticed.

"Like your friend Johanna—and her cleavage. How much of the audience would you say was Jewish?"

Cybill sighed. Not this again. "God, Quinn, I don't know! I mean, I wasn't counting noses!"

He gave a whoop of laughter, and she realized that he thought she'd made a joke. Well, maybe, unconsciously, she had! She joined in his laughter then said, "I guess it *was* mainly a Jewish audience. But what do you expect at a cultural event in Manhattan?"

"It's *exactly* what I expected," he said. "Why do you think I was so eager to attend?"

"Eager just to sit in a hall full of Jews?"

He raised his eyes heavenward, as if there could be no greater bliss.

She shook her head in exasperation.

The next morning, a Saturday, Cybill was at the stove frying bacon when Jesse said, "No bacon for me." Jesse had curly brown hair, a hawk nose, and a voice that often broke, as it did now.

"Why not?" she asked, wondering if she should pick his half-cooked strips out of the pan or cook them along with the others.

"I'll have his," said Daniel, resolving that dilemma. Daniel was blond like Cybill, with big brown eyes that he used to advantage. Jesse said, "We're Jews, aren't we? So we shouldn't eat pork."

"Oh, tosh," she said. "Those old dietary rules aren't a necessary part of being Jewish."

"They help remind us who we are," said Jesse. "I'm going to start keeping kosher."

"Just because you're fifteen, do you have to be so *predictably* rebellious? If you were raised keeping kosher, right now you'd be eating ham and shrimp."

"Perhaps. Still, I want to try keeping kosher. See how it feels."

"Jesse, you weren't even bar mitzvah!"

"Maybe I should have been," he said.

"You never made a peep about it then."

"Well, I'm going to keep the dietary rules. No pork. No seafood. No meat with milk."

"I hope you don't expect me to get new set of plates and silverware."

"No, Mom. We don't have to overdo it. I'm not suggesting separate refrigerators and dishwashers. And don't cook any special substitutes for me. I can always fill up on bread and peanut butter."

"Whatever you say."

Daniel ate his four pieces of bacon one after the other, before he ate his eggs. Then he asked, "Mom, how old is Quinn?"

Her sons had met Quinn for the first time the night before, when he had picked her up from her house, instead of meeting her elsewhere as she had insisted he do before.

She said, "Why do you ask?"

Daniel said, "He seems so much younger than Daddy."

She said, "He isn't as young as he looks. He just has this very young face."

Jesse asked, "So how old is he?"

She said, "Oh . . . he's in his thirties."

"Thirty-*what*?" demanded Jesse.

Cybill saw that resistance was futile. "He's thirty-two."

Jesse was scandalized. "Ma – he's fifteen years younger than you are!"

She said, "I can do the math, sweetie."

Jesse said, "But that's so weird."

"Not really. Men often date younger women, and women sometimes date younger men."

"But fifteen *years*. Ma!"

"Well, he doesn't have a problem with it, so I don't either."

"Whatever," said Jesse. And then he touched the crown of his head, pulled his ear, and brought his hand down again. Daniel giggled and did the same thing, more clumsily.

"Don't be cruel," she said.

"But what's *with* it?" Jesse asked.

"It's a tic. We haven't discussed it."

❊ ❊ ❊

When she called Quinn at home midweek to tell him what to wear for the seder, she heard the television in the background. This was unusual; she knew Quinn didn't watch much TV. And it wasn't a sports show—she could tell, by the sporadic laughter, that it was some kind of sit-com. She could just make out the main character's voice: female, familiar, unpleasantly nasal. A horrible suspicion seized her. "Quinn, what are you watching?"

"Some silly sitcom."

"*What* silly sitcom?"

"I don't know." He paused. "'The Nanny,'" he admitted.

"Quinn, you've gone too far!" The comedy featured a grating, loud-mouthed Jewish heroine.

"It's funny!" he protested.

"And I suppose you think Fran Dreschler's the most beautiful woman in the world?"

"No," he said sincerely. "You are."

How could she stay mad at Quinn when he said things like that?

❈ ❈ ❈

Quinn and Cybill were sitting on a sofa in Scarsdale. She had never seen Quinn dressed in a suit before, and she thought he looked quite wonderful. Instead of being a guitarist in a folk band, perhaps he should have been a male model. Quinn seemed equally delighted by her own appearance. She wore a fitted blue suit with no blouse. A single pearl nestled in the hollow of her neck. "You look beautiful," he whispered. "But why didn't you wear your Star of David?"

She whispered back, "I didn't want to get you hot and bothered."

Quinn smiled. He had his hand on her shoulder and his fingers strayed onto her neck. This was fine with Cybill. When he was touching her, he never scratched his head and pulled his ear. By now she had learned that his head-scratch, ear-tug tic was largely unconscious and only done with his right hand. If he was holding something in his left hand, his right hand would go through the motions, but if he held something in his right hand, he never did the moves. Oddly, touching her with either hand also kept the tic in check. She still had not spoken to him about it. Since as a guitarist he was usually holding something in his right hand, the tic did not impede him artistically, but it was awkward socially.

She looked around the living room. Her aunt Lillian was carrying a platter of pickled turnips and cauliflower to the coffee table, and her cousin Susan emerged from the kitchen with a bowl of her mother's famous chopped liver. Her uncle Moses was passing out yarmulkes. Their son, Sammy, now known as Shmuel, wore a knitted yarmulke fulltime so he didn't need one of the satin ones Uncle Moses was distributing. Shmuel was a newly orthodox accountant who left his job at two every Friday afternoon to have plenty of time to get home before the Sabbath. Shmuel, she knew, exasperated and embarrassed her sophisticated aunt and uncle, who had to buy new sets of glassware and silverware so their son could eat with them on visits. Their other children, Cybill's cousins Bill and Susan, were as comfortably easygoing in their Judaism as their parents. Lillian and Moses let it be known that they thought Shmuel was going too far. He insisted that his wife, Adele, follow the orthodox tradition and shave her head and wear a wig. For women with mousy hair, the wig improved their looks, but Adele's hair had been glossy, thick, and dark. He probably insisted that she go to a *mikvah* every month.

Now Adele was on the couch, dandling her youngest child (she had three under age three). Cybill's mother, Rochelle, was chatting with Rain. Daniel and Jesse were trying to see something that Willow, Susan's thirteen-year-old daughter, was holding behind her back. Willow ran out of the room and up the stairs, closely followed by Jesse and Daniel.

Quinn whispered, "It's hard to believe that your mother and your aunt Lillian are in their seventies."

"You're not supposed to know how old they are," she whispered back. "In fact, my mother expects me to lie about my age so no one will guess *her* age."

"How old are you supposed to be?"

"Thirty-six."

"You'd still be older than me."

"What are you love-birds whispering about?" asked Susan.

"Age and youth," Cybill said. Quinn tightened his hold on her shoulder.

Susan said to her, "Aren't our mothers amazing?"

Cybill said, "That's what Quinn was saying." Lillian and Rochelle were slender and strong and vivacious. By merely raising her eyebrows, either could command the attention of a roomful of people.

Quinn asked, "Are they typical Jewish mothers?"

Susan said, "Only in their love of food and family. They're much more elegant and glamorous than most Jewish mothers."

"And more intelligent," Cybill added. Aunt Lillian was a lawyer, Rochelle was an actress, and each said she would never retire.

"Bodes well for you," said Quinn to her and Susan.

"Oh, I can't possibly live up to my mother," said Susan.

Cybill said, "Nor I. Last week she beat me at tennis—singles!"

"We're ready," announced Uncle Moses, and they all trooped into the dining room, where the long table had been festively set. The china was edged in gold, and the napkins were edged in lace. There were silver candlesticks and vases of low flowers down the middle of the long table. There were several glasses and plates at each setting, with a Haggadah, the Passover prayer book, on the top plate. As was her custom, Lillian had made place cards for her guests, and everybody milled around until they found their places and sat down.

Cybill took her place beside Quinn at the table. He put his hand upon her knee, and she felt a surge of happiness, as she always did when he laid hands upon her. Whenever they touched, she felt, instantly, about 30% happier than before. Perhaps he did, too, and this blunted his need to scratch the top his head and check that his ear was still there.

Uncle Moses, at the head of the table, began to speak. "Tonight, we commemorate the exodus of the Jews from Egypt. All over the world, Jews are celebrating this liberation from slavery and educating others about it. I understand this is Quinn's first seder."

Quinn bobbed his head at this acknowledgement and squeezed Cybill's knee.

Uncle Moses continued. "Lillian has spent days cooking us a marvelous feast, and the tantalizing aromas are wafting to our nostrils at this very moment. But the most important part of this evening comes before we can take up our knives and our forks."

"Not true!" said Susan, who had helped with the cooking.

Moses ignored his daughter's outburst, merely saying, sternly, "Let us read from the Haggadah."

As a little girl, Cybill had found this pre-dinner reading and praying excruciatingly long. Then when she was fifteen, she had timed it and had been astonished to learn it took only half an hour. The longest half hour of the year!

Uncle Moses intoned, "Would you please turn to page three." She looked over to Quinn's Haggadah and saw that she didn't have to tell him to open the book backward—reading right to left—for he was already doing so, a smile playing on his lips. Her tall Norwegian! The red satin yarmulke looked ridiculous upon his bouncy blond thatch, but he wore it with pride, as if it were a crown.

They read aloud from the prayer book, one by one, going around the table. When it was his turn, Quinn read loudly, with expression, as if from a pulpit.

By contrast, Daniel read the four questions softly and quickly. He had read the four questions with pride at age five, but now that he was eleven, he considered himself too old for this duty. Still, he was the youngest child who could ask the questions (next year Shmuel and Adele's Herschel would be able to ask them), and it was his role. "Why is this night different from all other nights?" Daniel read.

Cybill rephrased it to herself: "Why is this Seder different from all other Seders? Because I'm beside a tall and adoring young Christian."

Quinn was seemingly absorbed by the various rituals of the Seder dinner: Elijah's cup, the glasses of wine raised but not drunk, the symbolic hand-washings: the men mimed scrubbing their hands at the table, over their dinner plates. "Why don't the women wash their hands?" whispered Quinn. "Are they already clean?"

"On the contrary," she said. "We're considered so dirty we can *never* get clean."

"*What?*"

But Uncle Moses was frowning at their whispers, so she said, "Tell you later."

It was the thing she disliked most about the Jewish religion, this notion of women as being inherently unclean. This was, she knew, related to menstruation. Religious Jews sent their wives to a *mikvah*—a ritual bath—after each period. They wouldn't allow their wives to share their beds for a full ten days after menses had ceased. That was why in Israel, most hotel rooms had twin single beds rather than a double—to keep the men unsullied by their dirty women.

But if women didn't menstruate and ovulate, the entire race would cease! Cybill would get angry just thinking about it. And then there was the morning prayer for men: "I thank you, God, for not making me a woman."

After decades of terming herself an agnostic, in recent years she had taken to declaring herself an atheist. It seemed a bolder, truer choice. She was baffled by statistics on the number of people in the world who believed in a supreme being, and saddened to think that so many of her contemporaries were being drawn back to religion. She, too, longed for community, which synagogue surely provided, but she knew she would feel uncomfortable and hypocritical in a community of believers.

They were coming to the end of the pre-dinner prayers. As the Haggadah instructed, everyone was making chicory and *harosset* sandwiches on pieces of matzo, to symbolize the bitterness of slavery and the sweetness of life. Uncle Moses explained to Quinn that because they were Sephardic Jews, the *harosset* was made of dates, not apples. Soon, the beautifully set table was littered with fat, flat matzo crumbs. After a few more passages, came the words they had all been awaiting: "Serve the Festival Meal."

Cybill's mother said, "About time! Blessed art thou oh Lord our God and on and on and on and on!" Moses gave her a stern look, but Rochelle was laughing gaily. "As Rabbi Gamliel did *not* say, 'Let's eat!'"

This was their usual Passover dynamic—Uncle Moses, the host, pretending to be more pious than he was, and his sister-in-law, Cybill's mother Rochelle, merrily flirting with blasphemy.

Now plates of gefilte fish were being brought to the table— "Fishballs," she told Quinn—and there was that general hubbub that happens after people have been silent and constrained.

Jesse said, "Mom, I love gefilte fish. We should have it more than once a year."

Cybill said, "We could have it on July 4th. To symbolize the Jews coming to America."

"What's the pink stuff?" Quinn asked Susan.

"Horseradish. You put a dab onto each bite."

Shmuel said, "Could I have a glass of water?" and Adele leaped up to get it.

Rochelle said to Susan's daughter, Willow, "That's such a pretty sweater. The green goes so well with your eyes."

Susan said, "I picked it up for her at Bloomie's — 50% off."

Quinn said, to Cybill, in his jokey Yiddish accent, "Such a bargain! Such a deal!"

Except at that exact moment, all the little conversations coincidentally fell silent, and Quinn's mocking, "Such a bargain! Such a deal!" rang out loud and clear.

Cybill could have sunk through the floor.

Shmuel glared at Quinn, who covered his top lip with his bottom lip in anguished recognition of his awful mistake. He scratched his head, pulled his ear, rested his hand in his lap. Then repeated the sequence. He was starting on a third round when Cybill grabbed his hand.

Susan, who was serving gefilte fish, had frozen, plate in hand.

Even Rochelle, the actress and iconoclast, looked worried. She turned to Uncle Moses for guidance, as did most of the guests. They awaited the patriarch's response.

Uncle Moses looked shell-shocked. The silence lengthened. The tension mounted. Then Uncle Moses threw back his head and laughed heartily.

In utter relief, Cybill joined him. So did her mother, and Lillian — then most of the guests. Shmuel shook his head in mild indignation, but now his wife Adele was laughing along with the others.

It was, Cybill thought, the hilarity of release and relief. There would be no confrontation about anti-Semitism or permissible humor. Everybody would eat and drink and have a good time. The evening had been saved.

"Say something else," said Uncle Moses to Quinn. "You're good!"

"You want I should speak like this more?" asked Quinn. He hunched his back, shrank his large shoulders, and became an old Jewish peddler—albeit with Viking features. "You want a *goyishe* guy to become an old Jew?"

Uncle Moses giggled helplessly.

Quinn touched his beanie-hat briefly. Then he folded his arms and began rocking back and forth, *davening* as if in prayer. He gave Cybill a look of utter fulfillment, and she saw that whatever else she was to him, and whatever age she'd attain, first and foremost, she would be his Jew-girl.

Still *davening*, Quinn recited a phrase that had come up many times in the before-dinner prayers: *"Baruch attoh adonoi, eluhenu mellech ha'olam."* He gave her a look of triumph and joy.

Uncle Moses said, "Bravo!"

Cybill rolled her eyes heavenward—that is, toward the ceiling.

Quinn moved his thigh against hers.

4. ALAN ALDA IN MAMARONECK

1994

Being with Quinn made Cybill revaluate her marriage. Now she marveled that she had tolerated James's coldness, his gloom, his judgmental nature—year after year, decade after decade. The marriage that she had thought ideal ("We have the same values but different temperaments") she now saw as stunted and pale.

Now for the first time she understood the phrase she had pondered in Denver: "She thought she was happy, but she wasn't."

Over Christmas vacation, she told Rain, now a college junior, her new favorite joke.

A very old man and woman appear before the judge. The old man says, "Judge, we want to get a divorce."

"A divorce! How old are you?"

"I'm ninety. And she's eighty-eight."

The judge says incredulously, "And you want a divorce?"

The wife nods vigorously. "We hate each other."

The husband adds, "We've hated each other for years."

The judge asks in amazement, "So why did you wait until now to get a divorce?"

The wife says, "We were waiting until the children were dead!"

Cybill cracked up all over again, but Rain just stared at her coolly. "I don't think it's funny, Mom."

"Oh, Rain." Cybill shook her head. "I know it isn't easy—but you gotta laugh."

Rain said, "No, I don't."

"Well, I do." she heard a car honk outside. "It's Quinn," she said. "We're late for a concert."

Rain shook her head. "Why you're dating a man half your age is way beyond me."

"You exaggerate, dear." Cybill put on her coat.

"Well, he's closer to my age than yours."

"So? Do *you* want to date him?"

Rain opened her mouth in a scandalized O, and Cybill ran out the door.

Inside the car she and Quinn embraced fervently. Then, as he put his hand on the gearshift, she said, "We baby boomers may be the first generation in history to have children more conservative than we are."

She hoped he absorbed the message that they belonged to the same generation, at least according the statisticians, for their respective ages bracketed the standard baby boomer definition.

"Rain bugging you again?" asked Quinn as the car shot away from the curb. He put his hand on her neck, and she forgot everything else.

❁ ❁ ❁

Her divorce from James, fashioned by therapists, mediators, and gentlemanly lawyers (even hers, a female), was an amicable process. One provision of their separation agreement stipulated that each would speak of the other, to our children, with "respect and admiration." James was honest and fair about finances. The only object they argued about was a favorite omelet pan, for which they finally spun a coin. They filed their papers and waited a year.

When the divorce finally came through, there was no courthouse, no document, no ceremony. Just her lawyer's Westchester twang on the answering machine one day: "Your divorce is final now."

Rain was at college, Jesse and Daniel were skiing with James and Janice, Quinn was at a gig, and she was alone in the house. She played the message a second time, gave a little cry of joy, then left the house again.

She went out and bought a bottle of St. Germain (an elderberry liquor she had come to like), crackers, St. Andre cheese, and a small box of marzipan candy. She brought them back to her favorite room in the house, a small, glassed-in upstairs porch with a view of the water. She spread some cheese on a cracker and reflected upon how lucky she'd been to meet Quinn. Other middle-aged divorcees, she knew, were bitter and anti-male. Quinn had saved her from that.

She poured herself a second glass of St. Germain. She was glad the divorce was final. She was with Quinn now. In comparison with Quinn, James was old, fat, hairy and tired. Then she felt a pang. After all, James was also intelligent, successful, humorous, reliable. A good father. Prompt with the support checks. And he was, for his age group, attractive.

Still, aesthetically, sexually, and emotionally—game, set, match!—Quinn was surely the winner. Just thinking of his peerless butt . . .

Though there had been that great last time in bed with James. In fact, ever since that morning, the notion of another, favored woman had become an erotic mainstay for Cybill. Whenever she needed help coming, she would think, "He loves someone else even more," and, weirdly, that would do the trick. She felt ashamed that jealousy should be such a turn-on, but it was potent and reliable, and no one had to know about it, not even Quinn.

All in all, she thought about sex with her ex almost nil. In fact, she had little sexual nostalgia in general. Although she could remember past delights in some detail, she couldn't think of any former lover whom she'd want to bed again. Cybill was different now, and her former lovers would be, too.

And things were moving quickly and deeply with Quinn, whom she now termed, "My angel lover." He had an emotional depth that Mel lacked.

Johanna asked one night on the phone, "What makes Quinn so oddly besotted?"

"I've tried to puzzle it out. Perhaps he met me at just the right developmental moment. Like the gosling that follows the beach ball."

"You don't seem to mind."

"Being adored is surprisingly pleasant," said Cybill. "And it's certainly a change." Both from James and from Mel. Cybill felt sappy admitting that Quinn's devotion to her had become matched by hers to him. She felt radiant when they were together, and when they were apart, she never thought about Mel and the things they did in bed. Well—not often.

Johanna said, "I'm glad James was decent about the divorce."

"More than decent," Cybill said.

Indeed, Cybill's was much the best divorce she knew. Steven had been alienated from his daughters by his ex-wife, Suzanne, and now he ground his teeth so hard during sleep that he had to wear a special appliance to protect the remaining enamel. Wally was obsessed by his ex-wife, Alice, whom he'd ignored in twenty-four years of marriage, and he would call Cybill bitterly to complain that Alice hadn't sent him a birthday card or congratulated him on his latest book. Shortly after Richard moved out, a storm knocked a tree down on the roof of Nancy's house. Nancy submitted an insurance claim, and the company mistakenly made the eighty-six-hundred-dollar check out to Richard—who found the check, promptly cashed it in, and refused to let her have the money to fix the roof.

James and she would trade these divorce tales and congratulate themselves on having largely avoided anger, pain, and hostility — after the brutal months when their marriage was coming to an end. ("Because you took up with that woman"; "Because you didn't love me enough"; "How could I have loved you more than I did?"). Sometimes while James was collecting or returning the children, he or she would say, "We have to talk," and they would retire cozily to the porch, where they would sit on the love-seat and discuss some aspect of their finances or their children's well-being before kissing each other goodbye.

So when James brought Daniel back from camp and said, "We have to talk," she followed James onto the porch with some satisfaction. Jesse had just received the results of his Advanced Placement tests, and he had done very well. She thought that James and she would discuss how he should use the credits. Maybe he should skip a term at college —thereby saving them a bundle.

"Cybill," James said instead, "I wanted you to hear this from me and in person. But I haven't seen you alone in weeks."

"People travel in the summer."

"I trust you've been having a good time?"

She nodded. She and Quinn had just returned from Martinique, where they had exchanged endearments and declarations every waking hour. She asked James politely, "How've you been?"

"Janice has been so busy we haven't had a vacation yet."

Cybill no longer minded their living together, but she hated the idea of their vacations, of his traveling to wonderful places with a woman other than herself. James said, "Janice and I are going to Vancouver next Thursday."

"That's nice," she said. Cybill felt a pang. She had never visited Vancouver. Then she asked, idly, "Why Thursday?"

"That's what I wanted to tell you. On Wednesday, we're getting married."

Her heart, momentarily, stopped, but she observed herself behaving nicely. "Well, congratulations! I hope you'll be very happy."

James said, apologetically, "She really wanted this. You know how it is if you've never been married."

Cybill nodded—though Quinn, who had never been married, had never mentioned matrimony. Of course, Quinn was fifteen years her junior. She often marveled that she was with someone so inappropriate. Janice, however, was entirely appropriate for James: the right age, the right religion, and the right income bracket. By now, Cybill had met her several times, and although Janice was pretty enough, Cybill thought she lacked both heat and wit.

"You knew this would happen," James now said to Cybill on the porch, "when you insisted on finalizing the divorce. You knew Janice would want to get married. You made this happen!"

This was not entirely untrue. Now he'd be tied to her forever—bored for life—trapped in the bed he had made . . . Despite massive evidence to the contrary (like this impending marriage he had just announced), Cybill refused to accept that James might find Janice interesting.

She asked James, "How do *you* feel about getting married again?"

He shrugged. "It's a compromise. Everything is."

"That's not true," Cybill said passionately. "When I married you, I loved you with my whole heart—and that was no compromise! And now, if you'll excuse me, I'm going to go upstairs and have a good cry."

A single tear ran obligingly down her cheek. She had won the latest round in their continuing competition: *I suffer more than you do*.

❉ ❉ ❉

That evening, Cybill and Daniel drove to the Chinese restaurant to celebrate Daniel's return from camp. Jesse, who was still keeping kosher, was at his job as a counselor at a Jewish culture camp, and Rain was in Mexico with her boyfriend Artie, so it was just the two of them, mother and son. Daniel was thirteen. He looked like a child, thought like an adult, and acted like an adolescent, by turns sulky and exuberant.

Driving to the restaurant, Daniel said, "Mom, you owe me a memory."

"True." Lately he'd been expressing curiosity about her childhood, so they had developed a routine: each day she would offer him some childhood memory. At first it was simple, but after two months of this, it wasn't so easy to fish out new material. She thought and she thought.

"Go on, Mom."

"All right, all right, I have one! Now you may think this is odd, but when I was a little girl, my friends and I often discussed how we wanted to die."

"Gross, Ma!" he said appreciatively.

She continued, "We wanted a quick death, but not a disfiguring one, so burning, shooting, and drowning were out. Most diseases took too long, and involved pain, so they were not poplar options. Dying asleep, of old age, was pretty good, but it meant you had to forego bedside vigils and final farewells. We had long discussions about the merits of cancer v. stroke, the car wreck v. the earthquake."

Daniel snickered. "What morbid little kids! What did you finally decide?"

"We could never decide! The perfect death was certainly a problem, which was why the subject came up time and again."

He sat in silence, perhaps considering the question for himself. She was sorry to have led his thoughts in this direction. Changing the subject, she asked, "How do you feel about Daddy's wedding?"

"It's Dad's choice," said Daniel. "Do I have to get all dressed up?"

"No, it's just a simple wedding at her apartment."

"Are you going, Mom?"

"Me?" She smiled. "No, I haven't been invited. It would be rather odd if I was."

"Why, Mom? I mean, you know Dad better than anyone. Why shouldn't you be there?"

"Because it's supposed to be a happy occasion, and I can't, in all honesty, wish them joy. I don't want him back, but I hate the change in his marital status. I don't want him to be married to Janice! I want him to be divorced from me!"

"Mom, that's ridiculous!"

"I know that." Still, Cybill hadn't asked for any of this. Still, James left her for another woman. Still, he was going to *marry* her.

They parked across the street from the restaurant. The decor in the restaurant was minimal. The room was long and narrow, and the walls were beige and bare. Each table was covered with a white table cloth topped with a square of glass. People came for the food, not the ambience.

As soon as the waiter seated them, Cybill noticed the man three tables down and facing her. He was a handsome man with a full head of gray hair, and she figured he was probably about her age or maybe a little older. She thought, she should be going out with someone like that instead of Quinn. Quinn lifted weights and had big arms and a hard torso. He loved music, sex, and athletic pursuits. He had no financial or social ambitions, although he hoped to play at larger festivals and buy a fourth guitar. And whether or not he had full-blown obsessive-compulsive disorder, his hair-pull, ear-tug tic was certainly peculiar. When she once asked him about it, he said, "The drug I once tried for it lowered my sex drive," and she agreed that they didn't want that.

Glancing at the distinguished and amiable-looking stranger in the restaurant, she reflected that she should be planning for her future, dating someone she could marry, not rogues like Mel or children like Quinn.

Actually, she was enjoying her freedom and had often said she would never remarry. But that was before James had made his nuptial announcement. Now everyone would think he was more successful than she was, personally—as he had always been professionally.

The amiable stranger three tables down looked rather familiar.

"The dumplings," said Daniel, putting down his menu. "Then the beef with broccoli."

"Daniel, doesn't that man behind you over there look like Alan Alda?"

Daniel turned to look. "*Amazingly* like Alan Alda," he agreed.

Cybill said, "I'm going to have the spring roll and the chicken with eggplant."

Daniel said, "Maybe it *is* Alan Alda."

"Maybe."

"But what would Alan Alda be doing in Mamaroneck?"

"Visiting friends. Or relatives. Or maybe he's here for the golf tournament." The PGA championship was being held that week at the Winged Foot Golf Club.

Daniel said, "I don't recognize anyone else at his table."

Cybill looked. "Alan" was sitting with a middle-aged couple and a rather younger Asian woman. She said, "Not all celebrities hang out together."

A waiter came to take their order, and afterwards, Daniel asked, "Do you really think it's him?"

There as a momentary lull in the ambient noise level as several conversations paused at once—but not the talk at "Alan's" table. She could hear his voice distinctly. It sounded just like the voice she remembered from the movies and TV. "Yes, I *do* think it's him," she told Daniel.

"Mom, that is so cool."

It was better this way, Cybill thought. She didn't have to reproach herself for not dating a man like that—no one expected her to be going out with a movie star. He certainly was attractive in person—although not as glowing and buff as her adoring, unsuitable Quinn.

She looked at Daniel, who was permitting himself one quick glance over his shoulder at "Alan's" table. She said, "So why is it 'cool,' Daniel? Does it make us cool just to be in the same room with him?"

"Sure. Are you going to ask for his autograph?"

She burst out laughing. "Of course not! What would I do with it?"

At that moment "Alan" caught her eye and smiled directly at her, as if her merriment was contagious. Then he went on talking to his companions.

"Well, are you going to ask if it's him?" Daniel persisted.

"Why don't you? It's nicer if someone young does that sort of thing."

"I don't want to, Mom."

"Okay."

The waiter brought their first course. She wished that Daniel hadn't ordered dumplings, which she didn't like. She liked to share all courses when she ate out, and James and she had consulted about each dish before ordering it jointly. Quinn always let her have whatever she wanted from his plate, but his taste in food was different from hers — perhaps blander because he was so young. Cybill ate a segment of her spring roll.

Daniel said, "*You* do it."

"What?"

"Ask him if he's Alan Alda."

"I don't want to bother him while he's eating."

Daniel reached for a dumpling and said, "Michael Jordan said if he had just one wish it would be to be able to take his family to Disney World without being mobbed by his fans."

Cybill replied, "I don't think Alan Alda has achieved that kind of fame. He's a very good actor, and he supports all the right causes, but he's not a marquee idol." She dipped her next piece of spring roll into the sweet and sour sauce that rested in a small waxed-paper cup. "Anyway, I wouldn't go to Disney World if you paid me. Ersatz experience."

In Martinique, she and Quinn had gone kayaking and scuba diving. They had climbed up a dormant volcano on their hands and knees. They had danced on a wooden pier and made love on a deserted beach.

"I know what you mean about Disney World," said Daniel, "but it's still kind of fun."

James and Janice had taken the kids to Disney World a few months earlier. Even with alimony and her job, Cybill couldn't afford elaborate vacations with her children: she'd lost that competition with James, too.

Quinn made just enough money to pay his own way on vacations.

If she were married to Alan Alda, she could take all three children wherever she wanted. She would even be able to quit her job and find something more meaningful to do with her life. Create literacy programs for teens. Help channel micro-loans to third-world women. Work to close the local nuclear power plant.

The waiter brought their entrees. The chicken with eggplant was as rich and garlicky as ever.

Three tables down, "Alan" motioned for his check. Cybill said to Daniel, "I'll ask him on his way out."

"Are you sure he won't mind?"

"I'm sure. Anyway, actors love to be recognized. That's why they become actors in the first place. And it's not like he's mega-famous—like Harrison Ford or Pitt Brad." She waited for Daniel to correct her.

"Ma, did you do that on purpose?"

"Huh? Wha?" But she was over-acting, and he let the matter drop.

"So," said Daniel, "you're gonna?"

"I can't believe we've spent this whole meal worrying about Alan Alda! But yes. I'll ask. You'll see. He'll be pleased."

"What if you have something in your mouth when he passes our table?"

"Oh, I'll just casually spit it onto the table-cloth! Don't worry so much! It's just a simple question. And if it *is* Alan Alda, I'll slip him my phone number!"

"Mom!"

"Just kidding!"

"Why do you like to torment me?" asked Daniel.

"It's the devil in me!"

The devil in her wondered if indeed Alan Alda would find her attractive. Why not? After all, her young musician worshipped her. Quinn often declared, "You are my goddess of beauty and love," a sentence James could have uttered only sarcastically and which Mel would have modified pornographically.

They had settled the bill at "Alan's" table, and the four people stood up. She swallowed her mouthful hurriedly. "Alan," she noticed, had a bit of a paunch. But so did most men of that age. He was still a handsome, decent, talented man.

"Excuse me," she said as he passed her table. His companions continued on toward the door.

He gave a friendly smile and said, "Yes?"

"You look so familiar. Are you . . . Alan Alda?"

There was a moment's silence before he said, "Why yes, I—" Then he stopped, shook his head, laughed and said, "No, I'm not. But I wish I was!"

Cybill felt a blush in her cheeks. "You look like him," she said, sounding inane to herself.

"Sorry," he said, shrugging. Then he said, "Thanks" and moved on.

After he had left the restaurant, she met Daniel's eyes. He said, "You were good, Mom."

She said, "I feel stupid."

"No, you were fine. Are you going to finish that?"

She shook her head; she wasn't hungry any more. He reached for her plate, and she watched him eat. In the past year, he had grown four inches.

When he had finished, he said, "You know, I bet it was him after all. He said 'yes' at first. And, like, then he realized if he stopped and talked, he'd be keeping his friends waiting. So, then he said 'no.'"

Considering what she had always sensed about Alan Alda's integrity—but had she given the subject a moment's thought before tonight? —this seemed improbable. But she didn't want to disappoint Daniel, so she said, "You may be right. I should have given him my card after all."

"Mom!" Daniel was scandalized. "You're going out with Quinn!"

"Yeah, but he's such . . . an unusual choice. Not like Janice for Dad." She felt awash with regret. Why had she insisted on finalizing their divorce? There would never be closure with James, never!

"Mom," Daniel said patiently, "you have more fun with Quinn than you ever did with Dad. Quinn may be younger than you, but he makes you happy. You should be glad."

"You're right. So young and yet so wise." She patted his hand. "Yet . . ." she shook her head. Their waiter passed, and she raised her hand and mid-air mimed a scribble.

The waiter brought them their check and two fortune cookies. She didn't like the taste of fortune cookies, but she had never refused one, for she was always curious about the message within, and she felt that merely to crack the hard, sticky shell and not eat it was somehow cheating and would nullify the fortune.

Daniel broke his cookie and read his fortune silently. "This sucks!" he said and read aloud: "'Your lucky numbers are 8, 26, and 71. You will have a happy and productive life.'"

"That doesn't suck. It's what everyone wants."

"Yeah, but it's so boring and unoriginal. What did you get?"

Cybill bit into her cookie, extracted the slip of paper, and held it at arm's length to read it. She gave a yelp of laughter and read aloud to Daniel, "'Your lucky numbers are 7, 16, and 52. Do not trust a handsome stranger.'"

5. BEING IN BLISS

2000

This is our first day at the beach. Our first rainbow. Tango. Quince. This is the first time we've swum behind a waterfall. This is our first karaoke duet.

Over the five years they'd been living together, Quinn and Cybill had proclaimed dozens of firsts, but now the firsts were getting rare. So when Cybill's sister Lanie told her about a couples workshop called "Being in Bliss," Cybill went online to learn more. It seemed to be an introduction to tantra, taught by a couple from Boston who went around the country giving workshops. She thought it could be another first for her and Quinn—and who knew? Perhaps they'd learn something they could incorporate into their daily lives of rising for work and shopping for groceries and flossing their teeth. Perhaps they'd move closer to ecstasy.

Alone with Quinn at dinner, she told him about "Being in Bliss." She said, "I think we should do it."

Quinn raised his eyebrows as he chewed his steak. Then he swallowed and asked, "How did you hear about this?"

"Through Lanie."

"I don't get it." Quinn looked threatened. "What's it really about?" He put down his fork and swallowed some beer. Then he twiddled his hair and tugged at his ear. And did it again.

"It seems to be about 'namaste.' Or: 'The divine in me celebrates the divine in you.'"

Quinn said, "I thought you were an atheist."

"I can believe in the divine without believing in a divinity."

Quinn kept twiddling, and she did not reach to stop him. He said, "It sounds so California." Twiddle-tug, twiddle-tug. Twiddle-tug.

Cybill did nothing. Then on his own, Quinn stopped. He began eating again.

Maybe she should let him wind down on his own more often. Maybe the tic satisfied some neuronal need. Maybe she should just get comfortable with it—at least when they were alone.

Quinn said, "Anyway, I *do* celebrate you! We don't need a workshop for that."

"Maybe I need to celebrate *you*!"

"You do! You're wonderful."

"Thank you, darling. But, Quinn—this 'Being in Bliss' could be fun. Something different. It's only an evening. And if it's just silly—we'll have a good laugh."

"Well, okay—if you're determined. Great steak, by the way."

She scratched his scalp, and he gave a growly sort of purr and kept his head immobilized so she could continue scratching easily. She said, "I'm so glad you agreed. It's the kind of thing James would never have done. He was so set in his ways. We never tried anything new."

Quinn looked pleased at this.

She said, "It's great that you're so flexible."

"Anything to please the love of my life."

Cybill smiled. She could not imagine another human being loving her the way Quinn did. Certainly that rogue Mel McCabe and his 25 angel babies was incapable of devotion like Quinn's. "Being in Bliss" was something Mel would have liked; they had once done tantra together. She wondered if Mel was still with Gina, and if he had other women as well. What a lover he had been! Well, that was all history; she was bonded to Quinn. "Being in Bliss" offered a spiritual dimension and, perhaps, a new kind of sex.

On the night of the workshop, Cybill and Quinn and drove into Tribeca. Parking made them fifteen minutes late, and they rushed up the stairs, panting.

The door of the loft was open. Inside, a young woman with a nose ring sat behind a table collecting money. Cybill gave her some bills.

"Take off your shoes," the woman said softly.

Cybill took off her boots with regret. They were new red cowboy boots, and they gave her a couple of inches in height. "Put them in there," whispered the woman, indicating a cubbyhole against the wall, "then go join the group."

Her cowboy boots and Quinn's scuffed white running shoes shared a cubbyhole.

They tiptoed to the main part of the loft. The lights were dim. About thirty people were holding hands in a circle with their eyes closed. In front of the room, a gray-haired woman in drawstring pants said softly, "Drop your hands now, open your eyes, and form small groups of four or five." A gray-haired man wearing pants matching hers said, "If you're here with a partner, please join different groups." They were the leaders, Richie and Grace.

Quinn and Cybill went to opposite ends of the room. She joined a group of two men and a woman. One of the men sported excellent arms in a tank top. The other man, perhaps forty, had—what? Bell's palsy? His face was twisted to one side. The woman was about forty, too. She was dressed in leotards and a paisley-patterned diaphanous skirt. Cybill thought this was the perfect thing to wear to a tantra intro, and she regretted her own safe choice of jeans and a V-neck. But what a superficial human being she was, to be so hung up on exteriors. Surely this workshop was about finding and maintaining inner beauty.

She turned to see how Quinn was doing and was not surprised to find him sitting near a busty woman.

Grace said, "When you've found your group, sit down and introduce yourselves to each other and talk about your expectations for the evening. When you're finished, I'd like each group to choose a leader to summarize your remarks. Shanti, our assistant, will be coming around to see how you're doing." She indicated a tall man in the shadows behind her.

Cybill's group sat on the floor on brightly colored pillows. Lisa, the woman with the diaphanous skirt, was a stylist. That explained her wardrobe expertise. Lisa hoped the workshop would help her and her husband communicate their needs more honestly. Jerry, the man with the arms, worked in construction and was here because after ten years of marriage, he and his wife wanted to have hotter sex. Damon, the man with the face that drooped to one side, worked for a philanthropist Cybill admired. Damon was here because he wanted to know how sex could be spiritual. Cybill said she wanted to explore the concept of namaste.

Jerry said, "I guess now we should choose a leader." He gave Cybill a look.

She quickly said, "Lisa, why don't you lead?" Lisa looked pleased.

There was a gentle ringing from the front of the room: Richie held a little brass bell aloft. Richie said, "Leaders, please summarize the group findings and tell them to Shanti, when he comes around. Everybody else should quiet the mind and breathe slowly, steadily, letting your thoughts just drift by but not following any." He pressed a button and plucked strings rippled soothingly through the room.

Shanti walked to Cybill's group first. Suddenly, her heart began beating very fast because in the dim light as he gracefully moved toward them, Shanti astonishingly became her former lover, Mel McCabe. He grinned at her and said softly, "Hi, Cybill."

She felt the blood drain from her face. She couldn't say a word.

Mel, still smiling, said, "Remember—slow, steady breaths." And at that she remembered to breathe. He looked toward the others and asked, "Who's the leader here?"

Lisa proceeded to tell him their individual goals, but Cybill didn't hear a word. What was Mel doing in New York with Grace and Richie? Why did they call him Shanti? She had so much to ask him, yet how could they talk in this group, or even later, when Quinn would be by her side? She had never told

Quinn about Mel, and she didn't want to tell him now.

Now Mel, or Shanti, was gliding toward the next group and talking to the leader there. When he got to Quinn's group, she saw, to her horror, Mel/Shanti conferring with Quinn! It was a sight she had never imagined: the two men she'd felt the most passionate about chatting casually, oblivious of her.

She realized that it was entirely possible that Mel had figured out Quinn was her man. He might have seen them walk in together. Shouldn't Mel/Shanti be back in Boston working in his lab instead of talking in a low voice to Richie and Grace?

Richie stood up. He spoke to the group about their comments and led a general discussion about their hopes. Then he explained what one could expect from a week-end workshop. He said that the present evening was merely "a taste of tantra": a weekend, at four hundred dollars apiece, would provide a true introduction. "It will show you how to be transcendent and orgasmic *simultaneously*. Most of you here tonight have signed up for the whole week-end workshop — the others can still enroll."

She and Quinn had a wedding to go to on Sunday. Otherwise, Cybill might have considered it — if the fee had been lower, and if Quinn had agreed.

Grace said, "Now please close your eyes and dance in place, shaking your arms, moving your torsos, and letting the kundalini energy flow out." Richie pushed a button again, and "Brown Sugar" came pounding out and into the loft. Cybill danced in place blindly. This was fun! After a minute or two she peeked out. Mel was standing very near her, eyes closed, sniffing in her direction.

This was so disconcerting she closed her eyes tightly. Mel had always begged her not to wear deodorant, saying that the smell of her sweat was better than the chemicals she rolled into her armpits. Now in the loft, she couldn't remember if she'd applied deodorant that day and hoped she hadn't.

"Bigger movements," said Grace, and Cybill bent from the waist and waved her arms around wildly, hoping to touch Mel if he was still nearby. Apparently, he wasn't.

Grace said, "Now take these movements and this free, loving energy out to the floor. Open your eyes, move your feet and take great big steps out into the world!" It was childish and wonderful to be moving so largely among strangers. People were spinning and leaping and rolling on the floor. Lisa had her face upturned as if facing the sun. Damon was bent to the floor, swaying his trunk back and forth. Quinn was prancing and whirling his arms around. The room was filled with Dionysian energy.

Then there was silence. "That was wonderful," said Grace. "Know that this wild tenderness is in you always. It is in everyone. Honor it in yourself and in your partner." They bent their heads in silence.

"Now I'd like you to form two concentric circles," said Richie. He asked them to bow to the person across from them. Mel/ Shanti padded around, making sure that everyone was properly matched up. Passing Cybill, he gave her shoulder a squeeze which sank down to her center. Then he moved on.

She was partnered with Damon, the man with the face that drooped.

Richie said, "Now look very deeply into your partner's left eye."

When she stared at Damon's left eye, it seemed to get very big. As she kept looking, the rest of his face blurred. Damon's eye, she now noticed, was beautiful: a rich, chocolate brown. There was a melting eloquence to it, and if she didn't quite get his message, she absorbed its intensity. Richie said softly, "Now bow to your partner, acknowledging the divine in him or her before saying goodbye. Then the people in the outer circle will move one step to the right, so that everybody has a new partner."

Cybill's new partner was a chubby woman in a red sweatshirt. When she stared into her eye, it got very large. It was a gray and dreamy eye, and Cybill saw an island of serenity there. Richie's voice broke in. "Now say goodbye, and move on to your new partner in joy."

She was now with a knobby man who was totally bald. Despite

all this, he reminded her of her son, Jesse—that is, how Jesse might look in forty years. And as soon as she looked into his left eye, which was green, she was overwhelmed by its beauty, and by the man's frailty. He had once been as young and as hopeful as Jesse. She felt her own eyes fill with tears. Richie said gently, "Bow, please, and move on to your new lover."

Cybill found herself facing Lisa. Her eyes were subtly and expertly made up, but soon Cybill forgot all that and went deep, deep into Lisa's left eye. All else blurred.

After three more partners, Richie rang the little bell. "Remember all you have learned from staring deeply into the eyes of a stranger," he said. "Remember the transcendent beauty of each human being on the planet. Remember how we are all different and how we are all the same." Cybill felt her eyes fill with tears. Mel glided into her field of vision.

Richie said, "Please go to your pillows and lie down on the floor."

But giving Mel a look to make sure he was watching, Cybill quietly rose and went to the back of the loft, past the cubbyholes which held their shoes. Mel padded after her. She turned left and slowly went down a little hallway. Mel was still following. She went into the bathroom and he did, too. Cybill pulled a cord to turn on the light. Mel closed the door behind them. Then he took her in his arms and kissed her at length.

"Hello, sweetie," he said. "How's my angel-baby?"

"I almost fainted back there."

"I noticed," said Mel, with some satisfaction.

"What are you doing here?"

"I've been helping them out, as a volunteer. I love the vibe that builds in these workshops."

"Did you know I'd be here?"

"Not when I left Boston. But I looked at the list in the car. And wow! I was blown away! This is so cool!"

"And 'Shanti'?" Cybill asked. "What's with that?"

"That's my spiritual name. I use it for workshops. Have you missed me?"

She took a long look at him in the fluorescent bathroom light.
He had aged a lot in the last few years. His curly hair was mainly
gray now, there were wrinkles around his eyes, and his nose had
gotten quite red. He was a drinker, she remembered, as well as a
druggie. Now he hugged her against him so she was pressed up
against his shoulder, and she saw a woolly tuft of gray hair in his
ear, such as unkempt old men sometimes have. But Mel was only
forty-five. His biological clock was running very fast. Perhaps
he lived too intensely.

She said, "Of course I've missed you. But I'm with someone
now, and I try not to think about my rogue years. My years in
between."

"Your man's very cute," remarked Mel. "Seems like a nice
guy."

"He is. Are you still with Gina?"

Mel shook his head. "We broke up a couple of years ago. She
wanted marriage, a child, you know."

"Women," she agreed, although she had considerable sympathy
for the unknown Gina. It was perfectly natural to want kids and
to hope that the man you'd been living with wanted them, too.

"Yeah, women," said Mel. "So now I'm with men."

"What?" Cybill backed up. She felt the toilet at the back of her
knees, and she reached behind her to put down the seat cover.
She sank down on it and said, "I don't believe you."

"It's true though."

"But Mel," she protested, looking up at him in amazement.
"I've never met a man who loves pussy the way you do." Once he
had even opened her legs and shone a pen light into her vagina,
gazing, touching, licking ecstatically.

"Yeah, I do love pussy," Mel said amiably. "But I also love
cock."

She stared at him. It was true that he did look androgynous:
she supposed he always had. But she had never believed in
bisexuality, thinking that all female bisexuals were really
straight—and all male bi's really gay.

She said, "What does that mean, you love cock?" Perhaps Mel

only meant he loved *having* a cock.

He said, "Well, I like cock-play. Holding a cock, stroking it, rubbing it."

She thought: it's a buddy thing, no big deal.

Mel went on, "And of course I like having mine sucked. Gay men do it very well."

Cybill thought many straight men would like that. She asked, "But, Mel, do you like sucking dick?"

"Not much," he admitted. "My jaw hurts."

"Well, then!" she said happily.

Then Mel said, "What I like best about cock is getting fucked up the ass."

Her smile faded. "Well," she conceded, "I suppose that does mean you like men."

He really was bisexual! Once again, Mel McCabe was expanding her horizons. "You like everything."

"Yeah," Mel said cheerfully, "I'm a sado-masochistic faggot who loves eating pussy."

"I still find the faggot part hard to believe."

"I could show you," said Mel. "Maybe later tonight, you and your handsome young guy . . ."

She giggled. "Quinn? Not a chance."

"Aw. That would be fun."

"Get back out there," she said, standing up and giving him a little push.

"One more kiss?" Mel grabbed her hair, tugged her head back, looked fiercely down at her—then brought his mouth very gently to hers.

It had been this union of opposites that had so enthralled her once: his strength and his softness; his passion and his poise; his lust and his subtlety. His male and female qualities? Although initially incredulous, she now found herself imagining Mel kissing a man. He would be at once rough and tender—as he was now with her.

Mel straightened up; the kiss was over. She watched him slip out of the bathroom.

A minute later, she went back to the main portion of the loft. People were lying on the floor with their eyes closed; plucked strings shimmered through the air. She tiptoed across the room. When she passed Quinn, she heard him snoring faintly. Thinking about Mel's suggestion, she smothered a giggle.

She found a pillow and lay down on the floor, making sure that she couldn't see Mel. She closed her eyes. She tried to breathe slowly and bring down her pulse. But Mel had always made her crazy, and apparently now—grizzled, gay, or not—he still could.

✿ ✿ ✿

Quinn drove them home. When they got on the highway, she said, "It was interesting. How when we did that eye exercise it wasn't only men facing women but men and women facing men or women."

"I know," said Quinn. "I wonder why they did it like that. They could have had men in the outer circle, women inside."

"I think they wanted to encourage intimacy in general."

"Yeah," said Quinn, "but at the end they were saying, 'Please move on to your new lover now.' And that felt very strange."

She asked, teasingly, "Aren't you ever curious about what a man would be like?"

"No," Quinn replied.

"Why not?" Cybill asked.

"Because men don't have breasts."

She waited for more, but apparently that was the end of it for him.

After a minute or two, Quinn asked, "Shall we pick up some orange juice on the way back? We're out."

"Let's just go home."

A three-quarter moon was with them to their left on the highway. It followed them as they drove off at their exit, up the main road of their town, down their street and into their driveway.

Quinn turned off the engine. It was a clear Friday evening in May—not yet midnight. Neither of them moved to get out of the car. She ran her hands through his thick blond hair, which shone in the moonlight. She touched his soft neck.

Quinn said, "You know, the workshop wasn't as silly as I'd expected."

"I know."

"I expected more jargon," said Quinn.

"Me, too. I'm glad you liked the workshop. You seemed to resist the idea when I suggested it."

"I know. I felt like you wanted me to be. . . someone else. But it was really nice. Even liberating. And I liked their assistant. That Shanti guy."

Her heart began to pound, and her hands stopped moving on Quinn's neck.

Quinn went on. "He was really friendly."

"I bet."

"What does that mean?"

"Don't you think he was a bit . . . gay?"

"No," said Quinn. "He was just a nice guy."

She had never thought of Mel as "nice," but she didn't reply. "Nice" made him less dangerous, less riveting than he'd been—that and the tufts that grew out of his ears.

She didn't want to remember how obsessed she'd been with him.

What if she had somehow stayed with Mel—and then he'd decided to seek men? How demoralizing that would have been.

In gratitude to Quinn, she brought her fingers to his lips.

They gazed at each other by moonlight. "Moon princess," said Quinn.

"Moon prince," she replied.

"Our first workshop," he murmured, touching her forehead.

She smiled. "Who knows what we'll do next?"

6. CYBILL AT BURNING MAN

2008

"But why would you want to go *there*? Five days without bathrooms or showers? No beach, no historical sights, no restaurants! You call that a vacation?" Johanna was appalled.

"It gets worse," Cybill said, putting away the plates from the dishwasher as she talked on the phone. "It's supposed to be really uncomfortable: too hot by day, too cold by night, with these random, blinding dust storms."

"So why on earth are you going?" asked Johanna.

Cybill said, "If people go back despite these conditions, it has to be incredible."

"What does Quinn say about it?" asked Johanna

Quinn had an important gig in Boston on Labor Day weekend, so he couldn't accompany Cybill to the fabled arts festival in Nevada. Not that he wanted to. "Quinn is as baffled as you are," Cybill whispered into the receiver.

Johanna said, "For the cost of the ticket, and your flight to Reno, and renting that van, and the bike, you could get a week at a health spa and really relax!"

Cybill smiled. Relaxing was not what she had in mind.

Cybill was now sixty-two. She had heard about Burning Man from Parker, who was twenty-five. Parker was her daughter Rain's wild friend from high school, with tattoos encircling both biceps and spiky red hair. "Burning Man is like paradise," Parker had told Rain and Cybill on the back porch. "You exist in the moment. There's art all around. You live out your fantasies."

Turning to Cybill she'd said, "There are lots of cool people your age, too."

Rain had said, "All that dust! Artie has asthma. We could never go."

But Cybill had gone to the website and spent hours looking at photos and films and manifestoes. She found lots of reasons for going to Burning Man: the landscape, the costumes, the artworks. The spontaneity. The music. The ecological, anti-capitalist ethos.

And then there was the reason she never admitted aloud and scarcely to herself. One of the festival founders said in a documentary, "It's not just a sex party in the desert"—which meant, Cybill hoped, that it was. Quinn was a wonderful lover, but they had lived together for 13 years, and Cybill wondered if she might be, at heart, polyamorous. Weren't many people? Cybill had been relieved to learn that the most common sexual fantasy was group sex. She herself had concocted several potent scenarios on that theme. In real life, however, she didn't want more than one man at once—although sometimes she wanted one man besides Quinn, to make life more piquant.

Who knew? Perhaps Burning Man would provide a vacation from her virtuous life as a mate and mother and job-holder and Democratic Party officer in her town.

It seemed only a minor complication that at the last minute, her son, Jesse, who lived in Seattle, decided to go to Burning Man, too, with a theme camp called the Flaming Jews. After all, it was unlikely they'd run into each other by chance, in a temporary city of fifty thousand. He would be on the Esplanade with thirty people who juggled fire, and she would be camped alone somewhere in a Eurovan. She and Jesse agreed in advance to meet at Center Camp at noon on Thursday, and Cybill wondered how many other intergenerational reunions took place at Black Rock City.

She looked around her on the plane to Reno, speculating about the other passengers. Were any of them going to Burning Man? Most likely some of them, but she couldn't tell from their clothing or hair styles. She picked up her camper at the airport and bought a used bike from a special place set up for Burners. Then she stopped at a supermarket and bought groceries for five days. She drove through the desert and saw impossibly blue lakes in the distance. What minerals were in the water to give it such an unworldly hue?

After two hours, she got to Black Rock City. When it was her turn in line to be admitted, she was asked to step out of the camper. She gave her ticket to the man and woman greeters. He was almost naked, wearing shorts and bunny ears. She wore a bikini and a large hat. They each gave her a hug. Then he asked, "Is this your first time here?" She admitted it was, and the woman gave Cybill a little smack on the butt with a ping pong paddle, while the man said, "Welcome, Virgin."

Such a welcome! After that, she found a campsite, parked, ate a peanut butter sandwich, and crashed.

And now it was Wednesday morning, and she was waking up for her first full day at Burning Man, in her snug little camper with its pop-up top so you could walk around inside, and its cute little stove and sink and fridge, though the fridge didn't seem to be working so well. Cybill pulled a Japanese kimono over her nightgown and walked to the Port-o-sans, about a block away. They weren't as bad as she'd expected. Back at her camper, she washed and dressed. At home in Westchester, she'd been quietly accumulating Burning Man clothes and had devoted a dresser drawer to leggings and leather vests and camisole underwear.

Cybill still had a good body, though now, she supposed, more attractive clothed than in the nude. More from vanity than from modesty, she didn't want to get naked herself, and she had no intention of being part of the Critical Tits parade, not with her unevenly-sized breasts. Still, she liked being *around* nudity. That was part of this festival's appeal. A lot of the women went topless, and Cybill could vicariously enjoy being an exhibitionist, and a lot of men showed their butts, and Cybill could actually enjoy being a voyeur.

Cybill got dressed in leopard skin leggings and a coin belt and a tank top with no bra. She checked the fridge. Still warm, and the milk would spoil soon. She would go meet the neighbors and perhaps get some help. Cybill opened the camper door and stepped outside.

During the night, a young couple from Oregon had set up a little tent to her left, about fifty feet from her camper. Now they were sitting on camp chairs under the fly of their tent, holding hands, looking rapturous. They seemed so involved in each other or a drug that Cybill was discouraged from approaching them.

Immediately ahead of her, she faced the back of a large RV. There were many French voices on the other side. Cybill was both Francophone and Francophile, so she hoped she'd get to meet the hidden Frenchies. And now, from her right, she saw a man coming toward her, holding out a frying pan. "Would you like a Spanish omelet?" he asked.

"Me?" Cybill was surprised.

"Yeah. It's hot. I just made it."

"Well . . . *sure,*" Cybill said.

"I see you're for Obama," he said.

The theme of Burning Man that year was the American Dream, and Cybill had taped the cover of a recent *Utne Reader* to the door of her camper. It was a picture of Obama, with the headline "The American Dream." Getting him elected president was Cybill's American dream. Earlier in August, on her big back porch, she had held a Banjo Bash for Obama which had had raised $2,152 dollars for the Obama campaign.

"Of course I'm for Obama," Cybill said. "Aren't we all?"

"Uh-huh. What a cute camper."

What a cute cook, Cybill thought, for he was blond, tanned, with a white wolfish smile and a good body. Just a little chunky, how she liked men to be built. And, adding to his appeal, he seemed to be roughly Cybill's age, not a youngster, like Quinn. She said, "Come inside and take a look."

"I'm Troy," he said, stepping in.

"And I'm Carmella," Cybill said. She'd decided that would be her playa name. She loved the idea of a playa name. She loved that she was sitting here with this guy whose name might be Troy and that he would think of her as Carmella. She sat on a banquette, and he sat opposite her on the front seat that swiveled to face back. She took a forkful of omelet and said, "Wow, this is good. Thank you."

"I had an extra one," he said. "Anyway, we've been wondering about you. Are you all alone here?"

"Yeah," Cybill said. "I couldn't get any of my friends to come with me. They thought I was nuts." She didn't mention that her man couldn't come because of his gig. It seemed Carmella didn't have a man. "Who are you here with?" she asked.

"Oh, there are about ten of us, friends from Sacramento." He pointed to a muddle of small tents around a truck.

Cybill said, "I'm from New York." She observed that she and Carmella had that much in common, at least. "Hey, Troy, are you at all mechanically-minded? My fridge doesn't seem to be working. Although it worked fine on the trip from Reno."

Troy squatted to open the fridge and look inside. He put his hand on the carton of milk. "It's warm, all right. Do you have the camper manual?"

"Yes, it's in the glove compartment."

He swiveled the seat to the front and unlatched the glove compartment. He reached inside and got the manual. Soon he found the page for the refrigerator, which held instructions for changing the fridge from battery to propane when the camper was not in motion. "See, all you have to do is turn this switch," Troy said. He flipped the switch. They heard the propane firing up.

"Hey, that's great," she said. "Thank you."

"Did you ever think about looking at the manual?" Troy asked mildly.

"Actually, no. But I will from now on, I promise." To distract him from her ditziness, she said, "I just don't understand how propane can act as a coolant." Or did that make her sound even ditzier? Cybill took a last bite of omelet, relishing a burst of jalapeno. "Mmmmh. That was so good."

Troy glanced out the window. Outside, a woman in a jumpsuit was waiting. "Hey, I gotta go. Nice meeting you, Carmella."

He reached across and took her in his arms, and she felt herself relaxing into him. "I'll see you later," he said, and she knew that she would. Oh, this was a neighborly treat to look forward to . . . whenever.

She ate some bread, washed her plate, and began filling her backpack with the day's essentials: goggles and headscarf and sweatshirt and sunscreen and lip balm and two bottles of water and two joints and a lighter and a mug and breath mints and eye-drops and tissues and sunglasses and a peanut-butter sandwich and an orange and—she had to stop because the backpack was full. She went out to the bike and began pedaling along the street to the Esplanade.

At Parker's suggestion, she had camped by the 6:00 meridian to be away from the loudest music camps and to be centrally located. And now on her bike, she was part of the stream, the procession of people who invited you to look at them or know them before you moved on. They were people worth looking at. Cybill thought that Burning Man, by its nature, selected for the hardy, so most people here were in good physical shape. They were also into costume and adornment, so Cybill's head went from side to side and her bicycle wobbled as she admired one person or another. It gave people-watching a whole new dimension to know that you could say hello to anybody here and they would say hello back and probably talk to you and hug you. Or more. It was another world.

The landscape was alien from anything Cybill had ever encountered. There wasn't a plant visible anywhere: not one shrub or blade of grass: just sand so fine it was more like dust, stretching out in utter flatness to a circle of blue mountains. No leaves, no insects, nothing living. Was this what it was like when the ancient Jews had been forced to leave Egypt? Not an animal, not a leaf: all the land was beige. The lifeless landscape compounded her feeling that she had landed on some other planet. It wasn't like any camping she had ever done before, in green and private places: here, it was somewhat like a refugee camp, with miles of tents and vehicles parked in the sand.

But the tents and the structures were colorful and festive. There was always something to tantalize the eye: red sails, geodesic domes, tents made out of lacy netting, mutant art cars tricked out to look like telephones or spiders.

Beside a tent made to look like a cloud, a man on a chair called to Cybill, "Want a margarita?" She wanted to get to the Esplanade and look at the desert beyond, so she said "No thanks" and pedaled onward. This was the most difficult cycling she'd ever done, over furrows of soft dust. Yet when she got to the Esplanade, Cybill kept going: she bicycled out to the Man and then to the Temple and then she rode about from one art installation to another. Out in the deep desert, inside a sculpture of a dinosaur skeleton, a young man and woman were fucking, doggie-style. The man waved at Cybill. Cybill cycled on. It was incredibly hot, and her legs were aching from the difficult pedaling. The sun was blinding, even with her hat and sunglasses.

When she got back to the Esplanade, she got off her bicycle, exhausted. She went into one of the nearest tents to get some shade. She saw a sign: "Head Massage. For Women Only." A skinny bald man was giving a head massage to a young woman with very short hair. "Would you like to be next?" he asked Cybill.

"Sure." Cybill sank into some cushions and took out her backpack. She had smoked pot out there in the desert, and she sucked on a mint for her breath. She closed her eyes. She was so hot and tired . . .

She must have drifted to sleep because the next thing she knew, the masseur was touching her head very lightly, his fingers making circles on her scalp. "Are you awake?" he asked.

Cybill saw that they were alone in the tent now. "What a great way to wake up," she told him. And now his fingernails dug just a bit into her scalp, and she couldn't withhold a soft moan of pleasure. His hands moved from her head to her neck, from her

neck to her back, from her back around the front to . . . "Hey!"
she told him and sat up. "That's not my head."

"Oh! Sorry."

"That doesn't mean you have to stop completely," said Cybill,
flopping down again. He wasn't an attractive man, yet his hands
felt wonderful on her head. He massaged her scalp for another
few minutes.

Then he said, "You're a very desirable woman. Do you know
that?"

What could you say to this question? She didn't find him
appealing, but she loved his fingers on her scalp. Soon, as
before, he was extending the massage onto her neck and back,
and, once again, he tried to come around and touch her breasts.
"No, please," said Cybill, standing up. "I have to go now." She
grabbed her backpack. "But thank you. That was great."

She was glad to see another woman waiting for a head
massage. Maybe he'd get to cup a breast after all.

She got back on her bike, convinced she'd entered an alternate
reality. She had just let a total stranger pleasure her head! And
this morning in her camper she had given another stranger a full
frontal hug. What was making her do these things?

Just because she could. Just because she was anonymous.
Just because no one would ever find out.

Now she really wanted to find that cute Troy, but he was
nowhere about when she got back to her campsite.

The next day, she set off to Center Camp for her reunion with
Jesse. There were the usual long lines by the coffee bar, where
they were supposed to meet, and Cybill got out her ceramic mug
to be on the shorter line, for Burning Man was environmentally
responsible. After she'd drunk a cappuccino, she wandered
around. She listened to a jazz trio. She filled out a census form.
She looked at her watch. Jesse was now an hour late.

She decided to go to his theme camp, which was listed in the
program, so she got on her bike and set off. Ten minutes later, she
was at his beautiful encampment, fashioned from various shades
of flame-colored silk. She stepped inside the tent. A young man

with a yarmulke was juggling three zucchinis and a pepper, but he brought them down one by one when Cybill approached him. "Do you know Jesse?" she asked.

"Sure," said the kid.

"Could you try to find him? I'm his mom."

"How cool is that! Sure, I'll get him. You wait here."

Cybill sat down on a straw mat, and in a few minutes, Jesse came in. He had a wide leather bracelet on each wrist and a shirt with ragged arm-holes. He stared down at her. "*Mom*? What are you doing here?" She jumped up and they hugged. He seemed astonished to see her, although very pleased. His pupils were huge; his irises were narrow green circles.

Cybill said, "You didn't show up for our meeting at Center Camp today."

Jesse smacked his hand to his cheek. "Was that today? Gosh, sorry, Mom. It's so hard to make plans here."

She said, "So hard to *keep* them, you mean."

He looked into her eyes, as if she had said something wise. "*Keep* them, yes," he said. A chuckle bubbled out of him. "But *where* exactly does one *keep* one's plans?" He began to laugh some more.

"Jesse? What's up?"

"I ate all these mushrooms," he explained.

"Aha. Are they good?"

"Mom, they're *so* good."

"Well, I'm glad." She herself hadn't had mushrooms in twenty years, but she remembered them fondly. She said, "This may seem a little weird—but do you have any more of those mushrooms for me?"

He did, and she saved them for later. After she left Jesse's encampment, she biked back to her van. Then she cut up two avocadoes and sprinkled salt and lemon on them. She brought them round to the Frenchies, saying "*Aimez-vous les avocats?*"

Cries of joy and surprise! They did like avocadoes, it turned out, and Cybill got to use her French.

Later, she had an apple for dinner. It was strange being here in the desert: she scarcely ate, and she scarcely peed. And even though there were hot sweaty people in close quarters, no one ever seemed to smell bad.

Night fell, and the desert floor was pulsing. Cybill was going to dance, she had to dance. She put on her headlamp and got on her bike and headed off into the night, pulling up her flouncy skirt so it wouldn't get caught in the chain.

She got off her bike at the first place where people were dancing. She danced alone, but soon a tall gray-haired man began dancing beside her, a very handsome man with a hawk nose and piercing blue eyes. "You are sensational," he said. "What's your name?"

"It's Cyb. . . Carmella."

"Carmella? That's pretty. I'm Kirby."

"I've never met a Kirby before."

"I can be your first," he said, looking into her eyes.

Oh, Kirby was a charmer, and he knew it! I could fall in love with him, Cybill thought, absurdly. Soon they were strolling hand in hand from one bar to another. Cybill was sure that the number one drug at Burning Man was alcohol. Kirby said he was a film director from San Francisco. "Horror films," he said. She was surprised that he was so forthcoming, as it didn't seem the custom here to talk about your life in the outside world: "the gray world," Burners called it. But of course, Kirby could be lying.

He twisted the ring on her hand. "What's this?" he asked. "Are you married?"

"I live with someone."

"So where is he?"

"He's in Boston. At a music gig."

He squeezed her hand hard.

She said, "Hey! That hurts." She pulled her hand away from his.

"You shouldn't come to Burning Man if you have a partner. It isn't right."

"Why not?"

"We couldn't have a relationship."

"I thought Burning Man was all about the moment, the present. Anyway, even if I was single, you and I couldn't get involved. I live in New York, after all."

"That's true." Kirby's mood suddenly changed. "Come here, beautiful." And he pulled her toward him and kissed her. It was a delicious kiss. "Do you want to be my Burning Man girlfriend?"

"Maybe." She was thinking, *maybe we should kiss again.*

As if reading her mind, he brought his mouth down to hers and kissed her deeply and completely. Then he bit her lips. The pain was shocking.

"Hey!" she pulled back. "That hurt! Don't do things like that."

In response, he gripped her shoulder so hard she cried with pain. She said, "Let *go*. That's it. You are out of control."

He reached down and pulled up her skirt. She pulled away. "Cut it *out!*"

"You love it," he said.

Tears stood out in her eyes. "I do not. I'm going home. Goodnight."

"Suit yourself, Carmella."

"See you on the playa, Kirby," she said sarcastically. And she ran away from him, dodging tents and encampments in a zig-zag path. Fall in love with him? How could her instincts have been so wrong? She looked back to see if he was following her. He didn't seem to be, which was good. She didn't want him knowing where she was camped.

She was breathing hard when she got to her camper. She didn't realize she was crying until Troy came to her and said, "Carmella? Are you all right?"

She shook her head.

He asked, "What happened?" So she told him. He said, "What a creep. Give me a hug, you'll feel better."

After a time, they went into her camper. She said, "Would it be all right if we just sort of cuddled?"

"I love to cuddle," said Troy.

And that's what they did for the first two hours of that night, cuddled and talked, and then they fell asleep, and then they woke at dawn and reached for each other, and then things got serious, and seriously wonderful. She would open her eyes and see his wolfish smile and close her eyes again out of renewed excitement. This thrilling new man in her arms. His every move was sure and right, including putting on the condoms. He moved slowly and surely. She sighed. He seemed to like her, too.

Outside, the sky was streaked with gray and pink.

"Shall we go for a walk?" Troy said.

They saw many people on the road, people who'd been up all night. They were walking with their glow-sticks in their tutus and their rags. Cybill said, "Do you think *anyone* here voted for George Bush?"

"Probably somebody," said Troy.

"It's hard to believe," Cybill said.

He put his arm around her.

She said, "I'm so glad you found me last night." My Burning Man boyfriend, she thought, but did not say. That would be asking for a two-day commitment. Yet why should they look for other people when they were getting along so very well? They strolled around the playa together, investigating giant artworks. They returned to the camper for a snack and to make love again. They ate Jesse's mushrooms and giggled through the realization that they were all just chemicals anyway. Together, they watched the Temple burn, signifying the temporality of all man-made things, and afterwards, they danced wildly beneath exploding fireworks. They even exchanged email addresses.

※ ※ ※

A week after returning home, Cybill got an email from Troy. She read, with growing horror:

> Hey Carmella,
>   I misled you about something, and I have to set the record straight. I let you think I was for Obama, when in fact I'm for

McCain. I'm a life-long Republican and I voted twice for Bush. There! I had to get this off my chest. You are one classy lady and a total fox. I'm so glad we met!

Hugs,

Troy

Cybill gave a shriek of disbelief. This was worse than betraying her darling Quinn, worse than letting a stranger pleasure her head, worse than making out with a sadist who directed horror films. *This* was the Burning Man legacy, this was the after-burn, this was what living in the moment had wrought.

She had let a Republican into her body.

But, no, Cybill thought. She hadn't done that. Carmella had.

7. A FAN FROM ALABAMA

2009

Cybill invited him to have lunch in her garden because she thought he was somebody else.

After *Adultery Now*, the anthology she had edited was prominently and favorably reviewed, Cybill received many media requests and dozens of emails from readers. In her book, she described in detail and without judgment twelve extramarital affairs, chosen from hundreds her ads had elicited. Her readers responded warmly to the lack of condemnation in her book and to its understanding tone. Sometimes they described their own guilty or guiltless affairs. Cybill skimmed through a lot of these emails, meaning to go back and answer them. When she went on tour for two weeks, she fell further behind, and when she returned home, she still hadn't caught up with old emails of interest.

So when Cybill got a new email from a Steven Jensen that he would be in New York on a film shoot, she asked him to visit her in the suburbs. She did this because she was intrigued with what he had earlier proposed, which was to use her as an animated figure in a documentary about adultery. She loved this idea because of its novelty (herself as a cartoon character!) and because for this appearance, at least, she wouldn't have to worry about how she looked. She did not like how she looked on video, all darting eyes and roiling lips. She was better in stills, like the one on her book jacket.

This filmmaker, Steve, seemed thrilled with the invitation to lunch in her garden, emailing, "I'm so excited." Cybill pondered this.

He texted her from the 12:37 train, and she told him to look for her green Prius at the station.

The man who approached her car was young and extremely attractive. His hair was long and sandy. "I can't believe you invited me to lunch!" he said as he settled into the front seat of the car.

Cybill grinned at him. "Well, it's not every day someone wants to make a cartoon character out of me."

He looked at her with incomprehension.

Cybill felt herself blushing. "Didn't you ask me to be an animated figure in your film 'Apologists for Adultery'?"

He shook his head. "I just loved your book and wrote to you. Then I told you I was coming to New York from Alabama . . ."

". . . for a film shoot," said Cybill. "That's why I was confused."

"I direct commercials," said Steve. "We're on location in Brooklyn."

"And you came up here to see me?" Cybill turned on the engine. Was she flirting with this fan from Alabama?

"Well, you invited me, ma'am," said Steve. Was he exaggerating his Southern accent?

She pulled away from the curb and drove the short distance to her house. She felt his eyes on her profile the whole time. This was ridiculous. She was, after all, about twice his age. Yet she felt the right side of her face getting warm under his smiling gaze. She was smiling, too, as she pulled into her driveway. She turned off the engine and said merrily, "So this is all a big mistake!"

"A terrible mistake," Steve said, smiling. He held up a padded brown paper bag. "I brought you some peaches from Alabama. From my trees."

"All that way," she marveled. She led him into the house and put his peaches in a wooden bowl.

He watched her with a dopey smile, or so it seemed to her. A song lyric came into her mind, a woman asking a guy if he wanted her peaches, and if not, why was he shaking her tree? Did Steve want Cybill's peaches—or was he just thrilled to be with the editor of a book he admired?

Cybill was surprised to be getting email and offerings from readers. This was her first book; she hadn't considered that the readers might write back. But the book, which had taken a year to assemble, had hit a public nerve. Apparently, there were many guiltless adulterers in America. Take this guy, Steve. He had bought three copies of her book for her to sign. She thought: one for him, one for his wife, and one for his girlfriend!

Now he watched her closely in the kitchen as she put a bowl of salad and skewers of marinated shrimp on a tray. "I'll grill these outside," she said. It was a perfect June day. "Would you like any wine?" she asked. She had a bottle of Chardonnay chilling in the refrigerator.

"I prefer weed," he said, taking out a well-rolled joint. "Would you like to join me?"

"Sure, outside," said Cybill. She didn't like smoke in her house. Lately, she smoked only on weekends, but this was a special occasion. A fan from Alabama! A dashing young man who seemed dazzled by her presence. He snapped out of his daze to take the tray she was carrying. She opened the French doors and he laid the tray on the wrought iron table by the grill. She lit the grill and said, "Tell me about yourself."

He lit the joint and they passed it between them. Steve had married young, at nineteen, when he'd gotten his high school sweetheart pregnant. Now he was thirty, and they had three children and a pretty good life in Huntsville. He had to do a lot of traveling on location, and somehow . . . he fell silent and shrugged. Cybill suggested, "Somehow, when you're out of town, you're catching up on things you feel you missed."

He nodded. "It has nothing to do with my wife. I love Lou Ann, I really do. But . . . ! So when I heard you on the radio and even more when I read your introduction to the book, I felt you were speaking directly to me. Telling me not to feel guilty. That's why I wanted to meet you."

That and the photo on the jacket, Cybill thought. The sunset had given her face a warm glow. It had been a great picture, even before being Photoshopped. Cybill felt she was probably disappointing in the flesh. The veins in her hands, the tendons in her neck, the crows' feet . . . But Steve was gazing at her as if she were a mythical creature.

"I wanted to thank you," he said, looking into her eyes.

So, this was what it was like to be a distinguished older man! To have beautiful young women gazing at you like this! Who could blame those old guys if they sometimes took the peaches?

Cybill asked, "Does your wife know you're visiting me?"

Steve shook his head. "I keep your book at work."

"Who are the other books for? If you don't mind my asking."

"My friends."

Cybill turned the skewers to expose the pink shrimp with their appetizing black grill marks. She squeezed some lemon on them. She asked, "Your friends?"

"Yes, Jason and Zeke. They think it's amazing that someone comes right out and says what you say in the introduction. Especially a woman."

"Whatever people hide tends to be interesting," said Cybill, "so I assembled some stories about adultery."

He took out his phone and quickly typed what she had said. She asked, "Is this an interview?"

"No, ma'am! But you sound like a writer even when you're making lunch!"

"You sure know how to flatter a girl," she said, smiling at the absurdity of "girl."

They sat down to eat. Apparently, she could do no wrong today. The shrimp were crisp yet moist, and she let out a little "mmmm!" Steve didn't seem to notice the food. He asked, "Are your kids okay with your book? I mean, their mom talking about adultery in the introduction."

"Oh, they hate it!" she replied. "But they have their father's last name, so they're not directly humiliated."

"And the Dad?"

"Obviously, he hates it, too. But he's irrelevant. We've been divorced for many years. And later I learned he was having romantic adventures throughout our marriage."

"'Romantic adventures,'" mused Steve. "I like that."

"Male gay couples are much more tolerant of that sort of thing," Cybill said. "They know that true love doesn't necessarily mandate fidelity. They seem to be less jealous if their partner has a fling. Some of them have open relationships."

"Well, maybe gay men," said Steve. "It wouldn't work for heterosexuals."

"Don't be so sure! In France, marital infidelity used to be commonplace. People would have little apartments just for that, for the '*cinq a sept.*'"

Steve looked puzzled so she added, "Five to seven, at the end of the day. When lovers could see each other, after work and before going home. It was practically institutionalized! When Mitterand was buried, his wife and his mistress were in attendance at the gravesite."

"No way," said Steve.

"Way!" said Cybill. She found herself warming to her subject. "It's all about framing the discussion, establishing a new vocabulary. Most women don't have many opportunities for adventure. Most men don't, either. Adultery is all about adventure. Emotional and sexual thrills. Uncertainty. And risk! Does he really love me? Will anyone ever find out? No danger, no thrill."

"But what about marriage?"

Cybill finished her mouthful of salad. "A good marriage is a wonderful thing, but it rarely provides sexual and emotional thrills. Some people—not all people—just need romantic excitement, ecstatic encounters, sexual novelty. I happened to collect these stories about women and men who wanted more romance in their life . . ." The top of her head was buzzing. "I'm very high," she said. "That's good weed."

"That's also from my garden." He took out the roach and relit it. When he offered it to her, she waved it away. "I'm fine."

He said, "So how does it feel to be an apologist for adultery?"

Cybill said, "I have to admit it's been fun." She looked into his eyes before adding, "Exciting." She looked away. Oh, you are bad, she told herself.

He said, "And when did you last commit adultery?"

"Too long ago," she murmured. "Would you like some coffee?"

"What did you say?"

"'Would you like some coffee?'"

"No, before that."

"I don't remember," she lied. "I'm putting some coffee on for me and I'll put some on for you." Sometimes it was better not to give choices, best to just assume control. But who had control here? The one who held the power usually made the first move, so who, if anyone, should initiate any action? He because he was the man? She because she was the elder? He because he was the Beauty? She because she was the Author?

They fell silent in the kitchen. Cybill measured and ground beans and put them in the filter. She filled the well with water. She pushed the button so it glowed orange.

He came to her from the back, wrapping his arms around her shoulders. She kept utterly still, gratitude flooding through her. She turned to face him. Her eyes sought and received confirmation from his before his lips moved down to meet hers.

Oh, mouths, the ways lips and tongues could press and retreat, dart and caress, harden, mash, and soften in the quest for communion! They were on the living room couch now, and Cybill thought why stop? He smelled young and fresh, and he offered her worship. And tonight Quinn wouldn't be home until six.

Steve certainly knew all the moves. She had to make him stop because she wanted to come with him inside her, and when he pushed into her, she did. He was pretty quick himself.

They looked at each other, delighted.

He said, "Oh my God."

She said, "I know."

"I'm not usually so fast," he apologized.

"Nor I," she lamented.

They burst out laughing.

She said, "I guess we excite each other."

He said, "I've never banged an author."

She said, "I've never banged a fan."

He said, "Tell you what. Let's smoke and fuck some more."

When she heard that word, she felt lust all over again, and the second time was longer and more varied than the first, and even better. They fell into a light doze.

Steve woke up first. He looked at his phone. "Hey, I have to get back to Brooklyn. There's a crew meeting at eight."

She eased out from under him. "I'll take you to the next train." She went to the bathroom and smiled at herself in the mirror. Oh, yes, she had the glow! She washed her face and brushed her hair. She put on a little makeup.

She was sorry he lived so far away, in Alabama. Or could this ever be an ongoing affair, no matter where he lived? Ben Franklin wrote that men should always flirt with older women, "because they are so grateful." She wouldn't want a relationship like that, based on gratitude. Yet . . .

She returned to the bedroom. "My turn," Steve said, going to the bathroom in his boxers.

Cybill heard a beep and instinctively went to the phone, which was Steve's. An incoming message had just arrived.

Zeke: No way! That wasn't the bet!

Her eyes went to the top of the screen to read the whole thread.

Steve: Banged her! Twice.

Zeke: Whoo-hoo! How wazzit?

Steve: HOT. You owe me $100.

Zeke: The bet was for $50.

Steve: But twice!

Zeke: No way! That wasn't the bet!

Cybill put down his phone as if singed. That bastard, that braggart, that callow frat boy! Betting money on his charm! She felt totally played.

But did she have the moral high ground? After all, she had just read his phone, at first by mistake and then on purpose. She had invaded his privacy.

The next train was in nineteen minutes. Then he'd be gone,

back to Alabama, out of her life forever. She knew another woman would have called him on the texts, demanded an explanation, and sent him packing. Let him walk to the station if he had to! But she had always avoided confrontation, preferring to ignore or sidestep unpleasant things. She wasn't sure if this was good or not.

She called through the bathroom door, "If you hurry, I can get you to the 4:55." And through the bustle of their leaving, Cybill was able to pretend she hadn't seen the texts. At the station, she was even able to kiss him goodbye.

Back home, she found burnt coffee in the coffee-maker and a long roach in the ash tray. Alabama grass. She stepped outside and fired it up. Had she been altogether wrong about the awe she had seen in his eyes? Or had he been feigning fervor just to win the bet? And what kind of person even makes a bet like that? A brutish, boastful person. A cad.

But Cybill found herself smiling. She realized to her shame (oh, vanity!) that she was pleased that from afar he had wanted to "bang" her. O.K., the bet was degrading, but what is demeaning at thirty can be flattering at sixty.

And in bed they had been about twenty.

When she remembered that he'd written HOT, she felt herself get HOT again.

She noticed his peaches in the wooden bowl. She chose the ripest one and took a bite.

It wasn't as sweet as she had expected.

8. THE ADULTERY BROADCAST

2009

Cybill's editor called in great excitement. A popular host at New York's public radio station wanted to interview Cybill about her book. They also wanted to include two of the authors in the anthology—anonymously, with filters to camouflage their voices. Could Cybill contact them and ask them to participate? The broadcast would surely boost sales.

Cybill noted that the producer had selected contributors who were at the extremes of the adultery experience. One, Laura, lost her marriage and her children when she was discovered. The other, Amy, happily married, had a lover who brought her joy for twenty years. Amy agreed to participate in the program, and she lived in Connecticut, so she wouldn't have far to travel. Laura lived in Chicago and did not want to go on air with her traumatic experience. When Cybill relayed this information, the producer said, "Well, pick someone else then. Leonard wants two."

Cybill contacted Kim, who'd had several affairs and was having one now. Her writing was hilariously deadpan, and Cybill sensed she'd be a great interview. Plus, she lived in Manhattan. Kim asked some questions about the voice filter then agreed to do the show. In choosing Kim, Cybill was purposefully tipping the scales toward the positive, but this seemed only right after centuries when adultery was considered grounds for death—or, at least, disgrace and divorce. From the Adultery 3D to Adultery Now.

Cybill was happy that her book would get major exposure, and she sent emails telling her friends when the interview would take place so they could listen to her. She did not tell her children. The book was a sore point with her kids, even though she was the anthology's editor and not one of its contributors. Rain in particular thought it was an "icky" subject. Jesse opined that Cybill had only chosen it because it might become a bestseller. Daniel asked if her next anthology would be about porn stars.

Cybill did tell her mother, Rochelle, to listen to the talk. Rochelle had contributed to the anthology, but Cybill was under the strictest of orders to keep that a secret, even from Quinn. As a young woman, Rochelle had met a Italian in Rome, and every few years, on one pretext or another, she'd return to Rome to renew their bond. This continued for thirty years, and through Rochelle's two marriages, until the Italian died. Cybill thought that knowing about this affair (it was an open family secret), and seeing that it did not end in tragedy, had probably affected her own *laissez-faire* attitude toward adultery—that, and her coming of age in the hippie era of free love.

"Quinn," Cybill asked one night, "Does your mother ever listen to public radio?"

"I don't think so. She likes the TV. Why do you ask?"

"My interview . . ."

"I wouldn't worry about it," said Quinn. They had kept the book a secret from his mother, who was a practicing Catholic and did not like Quinn living "in sin" with Cybill. The book would outrage her. When she and Quinn left for her book tour, he'd said to his mother that they were visiting friends.

Cybill met the two contributors to her anthology for the first time in a coffee shop near the radio studio just before they were scheduled to go on the air. By design, they were all carrying copies of the book, which they signed for each other. Cybill told them about the format of the show: Cybill would be interviewed first, and then the host would ask Amy and Kim to join them. Kim was a stunning brunette in her early forties. Amy was about sixty, frumpy and dumpy. You didn't have to look great to have passion in your life, a truth that would not be evident on the radio. Cybill remembered once overhearing a haggard man of about seventy-five saying urgently into a public phone, "I can't see you now because my wife will find out." Cybill had been about thirty, and she'd been cheered that dalliance could extend into old age.

She had known since she was sixteen that adultery lay in her future. All the novels she loved were about adultery, and in her mother's European circle of actors and musicians, affairs were the norm. Marriage was for security and children; adultery (including Rochelle's affair with the Italian) was for thrills and romance. Cybill was surprised to find that her college friends and the friends she met later did not share this view. At first she thought that they agreed with her in their hearts, but in time, she came to understand that most of them truly believed in monogamy. She rather liked shocking them asserting she did not. "We should be like the birds," she would say to her friends (but not James): "Pair-bonded for life, but adulterous." DNA testing, she'd been pleased to learn, had revealed the true, promiscuous nature of birds.

Up in the studio, the sound technicians had Cybill speak into the mic to establish a level. Then the radio host walked in. He was older than Cybill had expected, and probably she was older than *he* had expected. Some days, she couldn't go a single hour without thinking about her age. His voice, however, was exactly as she remembered it from his show.

"Our guest today is Cybill Berenson, editor of the new anthology, *Adultery Now: Twelve Women Tell Their Stories,* which offers a new look at an old subject. Later on, we'll invite two of the contributors to join our discussion, but right now we have with us the editor of the book. Cybill, my first question to you is about the title. 'Adultery Now' seems like a call to action!"

Cybill smiled. She was aware of this interpretation but was prepared to gaily deny it. "Not at all! By 'now' I meant 'today.' These are *contemporary* accounts from married women who've had lovers. Women of today. Adultery has always been with us. It touches on our deepest emotions and inspires some of our best novels."

"That's because it causes problems," said the host. "No

problems, no story. But the introduction to the book, your take on adultery, seems to excuse infidelity."

Cybill said, "I would argue that the book is simply non-judgmental. Let's examine the subject without condemnation. Most of the women in my book have no regrets. Most feel their lovers enhanced their lives. But only anonymously can they tell you the unacknowledged truth."

"What truth exactly?" asked the host.

"That having an affair can be life-enhancing. Passion makes people feel alive."

"Adultery also ruins marriages, wrecks lives. Yet you're trying to take the stigma out of adultery."

"Something like that. Every case is different, but sometimes a discreet affair can be a harmless way to bring excitement to your life. Sometimes it can save a good marriage."

"Really! How would that work?"

"Suppose the partners got on well in every other way but had different sex drives. The more amorous one might feel frustrated if they were faithful but might flourish with a lover on the side. There's an example of that in the book, by a woman called Marie."

"But what about the moral compromises? The lying, the betrayal of trust."

"Most of the women in the book arranged it so they didn't have to lie, or only very rarely. But you have a point," Cybill said. "Life is a trade-off. Some women will sacrifice a little honesty for the thrill of an affair."

"This is a good note to pause on. We've been talking to Cybill Berenson about her book *Adultery Now*, and we'll return to this conversation after these words . . ."

An engineer turned off their mics, and the host said to Cybill, "Well done. Try to speak more slowly."

"Sorry." Cybill took a sip from the water bottle that had been placed by her side.

"Otherwise, you're great," he said. "OK, we're going back on the air." The host reminded his audience about the name of his show, who he was interviewing, and the name of her book. Then he turned to Cybill and asked, "What drew you to this subject?"

"I was a literature major in college."

"So was I. And I read a lot of war novels, but it didn't make me go to war."

Cybill's throat went dry at his implication she had "gone to war." She said, carefully, "I guess I'm drawn to the forbidden, the taboo. Writers sometimes need to say the unsayable. So I approached this subject to find out what the women involved had to say about it."

"Have you yourself ever had an affair?"

She couldn't believe he would ask her this directly! She said sharply, "Have you?"

"Well, I haven't edited a collection on the subject. I'm just trying to get a sense of what got you interested. You don't have to answer the question."

"No, no," Cybill said, surprising herself. "I suppose you have the right to ask. Once, early in my marriage—we've been divorced for many years—I came close. This was thirty-five years ago and sex was in the air."

"So who was he?"

"He was a former professor of mine, an English teacher, and we met by chance at a reading."

"It's always the English teacher," observed the host, "and never the chemistry prof. Why do you suppose that is?"

"Books open us up, make us talk about intimate things! Books depict longing and intensity. Books are passion-adjacent! When I met my teacher again, he seemed super forbidden and super exciting. So we, uh, made out a bit. But I pulled back. I found I just couldn't. And after that I began having children."

"Yes, I see you have three children. How do they react to your book?"

"They don't like it. But they're adults now. I don't live to please them."

"And you're not married now . . . ?"

"No, I live with someone, though. We've been living together fourteen years."

"And what are his thoughts about the book?"

"I don't know. I've never asked."

"He might mind living with an apologist for adultery. Or isn't it adultery if you aren't legally married?"

Cybill paused before answering. "A marriage certificate is irrelevant, either way. But it isn't an issue." I've been faithful, she thought. Except for Troy at Burning Man. And Steve from Alabama. But each had been temporary and neither any threat to Quinn.

The host asked, "So what about open marriage?"

"That would seem to be the best of both worlds, right?" said Cybill. "Have you ever read a book called *The Ethical Slut*?" Years before, Cybill had read it at Mel's behest.

"I missed that one," the host said drily.

"Well, the author says that there's nothing wrong with having more than one lover at once, as long as everyone is honest about it. And that's where open marriage comes in. It's a great idea, but it rarely seems to work out. There's just too much jealousy. Maybe discretion is better. Maybe all secrets aren't bad. Maybe they add mystery to life. Maybe they help keep us sane."

"Maybe you're right," said the host. "So many maybes! I've been talking to Cybill Berenson, the editor of the controversial collection *Adultery Now*, and after a brief break we'll be talking to two of the women who have pieces in the collection. Because both women are married, we'll be using voice filters to camouflage their voices."

The sound technicians turned off the mics again. "That was good," said the host.

Cybill nodded. She found her shirt was wet under the arms. How had he done it? Gotten her to talk about that English teacher? What if he were listening? She let Amy and Kim answer his questions in the second part of the broadcast; she herself contributed little. Amy was consistently pleasant, and Kim was just as dry and wry in conversation as she was in prose.

※ ※ ※

When Cybill got home, she saw Rain's car in the driveway. She ran into the house. "Rain?" she called.

Rain came clattering down the stairs. For such a slim woman, she had a heavy tread. Her face was white and her eyes were furious. "I can't believe what I heard on the radio," she said. "I'm driving along in my car, and suddenly I hear my *mother* talking about making out with her English teacher! Or maybe it was more than making out."

"It wasn't, Rain. Why are you so upset?"

"You said it was early in your marriage! And I was born three years after you got married. Is Daddy even my father?"

Cybill snorted. "Of course he is! Have you ever looked at your profile?"

"Maybe you've been saying I have Daddy's nose all these years just to fool me!"

"Am I the only one who's said it?"

Rain was silent. She really did have James's nose. Finally, she said, "Maybe I'll get a DNA test."

"Do what you want," said Cybill, "but James is your father. I didn't sleep with the English teacher. And, yes, I had a life before you were born, and I've edited a book you don't like. I'm still your mother."

"How could you cheat on my father?"

"Oh, please. Don't get so pious. It turns out that your father fooled around plenty himself."

"He did? And you didn't mind?"

"I only found out when we were getting the divorce."

"Well, I think you're both disgusting," said Rain.

"No we're not. We were young. We gave in to passion. And it was the seventies. And eighties."

"You betrayed each other!"

"We didn't see it like that. For me, it didn't have anything to do with James. It was all about . . . the other person. And intensity."

"That English teacher? He should lose his job!"

"Rain, I wasn't his student any more. I was in my twenties. I was dazzled by his erudition. And we didn't go all the way."

"I suppose he was married, too?"

Cybill nodded.

"Oh, you're *all* disgusting, all of you!" And she grabbed her coat from where she'd thrown it over the banister and slammed the door behind her.

Cybill knew that now she'd be hearing from Daniel and Jesse, for Rain would be sure to tell them. God, what was with this generation? Such prudes. She should send them each a copy of John Updike's *Couples*. She went into the kitchen to start cooking dinner.

Quinn came into the kitchen. "That sounded bad," he said.

"She can be such a little . . . *Puritan!*"

"She heard the broadcast?"

"Yeah. She was driving along in her car . . ." Cybill opened the refrigerator door and began rummaging through the vegetable bin.

"Well, what did you expect?"

Cybill found the fennel bulb.

"I didn't expect her to listen to the show!"

"You didn't have to confess to that near-affair or whatever."

"I know, Quinn. Now I'm sorry I did. But it was so long ago! And, you know, it gives my book more credibility." She put the cutting board on the counter.

"Your book!"

"Yes, my book! I'm finally getting a little recognition and the book is important to me." She didn't mention the money, which was good but not great. Her book hadn't made any bestseller lists, except for a niche one on Amazon. "These women in the book demonstrate that adultery can be joyful! It doesn't have to destroy your life or your self-worth. People need to hear that message." She took the knife down from the rack.

Quinn said, "Women are usually less tolerant about it than men."

"You're right. In the movies, at least, the standard reaction of a wife who discovers her husband is having an affair is to throw all his clothes out the window."

Quinn laughed. "And it's always a second-storey window."

She began cutting the fennel for a citrus salad.

"Would you throw my clothes out the window?" Quinn asked, smiling.

"Of course not. Would you throw mine?"

"Just that long purple dress you wear all summer long."

"You never told me you didn't like it."

Quinn shrugged.

"Anyway," said Cybill, "none of that is relevant to you and me." She wondered how Quinn would take the "that." Would he assume it meant she'd been faithful? Or would he think that for enlightened people like them, conventional morality (throw away the clothes! throw away the marriage!) was irrelevant? She got an orange and a grapefruit from the fridge. "Quinn, the host asked me how you felt about this book, and I realized I didn't know. You never told me."

For a while, Quinn was silent.

She prompted, "Yes?"

"I think you're doing what you have to do," he said at last. "And it's not so important how I feel."

"It's important to me," Cybill said.

"Well, to be honest, I'm worried about my mom finding out."

"That's it?"

"Yeah. Besides that—it's your gig and you're having fun with it. Fine with me."

"You're not embarrassed?" Cybill looked up from her cutting board.

He waggled his head slowly back and forth. "Maybe a teenchy bit. But it's a good book, maybe an important book. You needed to do it."

She put down her knife and threw her arms around him. "I must have been very good in a past life to get such a great guy as you."

"No, no, *I* was the good one."

9. THE FACEBOOK LOVER

2010

Cybill was new to Facebook, and until she met Lucas, it held little appeal for her. She regarded it as homework: once a week she forced herself to log in, mainly to get news of her children. But after meeting Lucas, Facebook assumed a whole new importance. Now she went there every day, sometimes more than once. For the first time, she found herself commenting on her friends' posts, which led to other comments, all of which she was notified about in her email, all of which she responded to by clicking the link to follow the conversation trail. Just imagining Lucas reading her remarks and speculating about her, as she did about him, charged every word with significance, although she did not know whether, in fact, Lucas got to see her comments on the posts of her friends. Cybill remained puzzled by the Facebook architecture: she'd have to ask Jesse to explain it. Lucas had made the entire subject a lot more intriguing.

Cybill first met Lucas at an environmental conference in Bedford. Cybill wandered into a small auditorium and heard a man talking about his job: helping people work with their local officials on climate change issues. Lucas spoke with energy, passion, and humor. Later, she asked him for advice about the Green Expo she was organizing in her town. This was the first time such an event would take place: a kind of trade show for those providing and seeking environmental services, from mindful landscaping to solar energy. Indeed, ten solar energy companies had taken tables. How could she persuade the mayor and the trustees to get behind her efforts?

Lucas laughed. "That's the easy part. You'll see. Green is very trendy now, green or green *washing*. Anyway, just give your mayor a chance to give a speech and he'll support you 100%."

Cybill was glad to say, "It's a she."

Lucas held up his hands in mock horror. "Oh my God! Revealed as a chauvinist!"

"You said it, not me," Cybill said, hearing flirtation in her voice. Huh? Lucas had a patchy gray beard, crooked teeth, and a soft belly. His eyes were fine, large and hazel, but one of them sometimes wandered. It didn't matter. Cybill was inexplicably drawn to him. They exchanged cards, and she saw that he lived across the county, thirty miles from her. The next day, he friended her. In the days that followed, every time she saw him on Facebook, the front of her body heated up. And at her age, too.

Sometimes she felt like she was in junior high, commenting on Lucas's wall and flirting with him publicly online. His Facebook friends—at least those who responded to his frequent posts— were overwhelmingly female, and when Cybill joined their ranks it felt like she was throwing down the gauntlet. She always clicked on the photos of these other women, these Facebook friends of his, to enlarge the pictures and measure herself against them, which was childish of her, or worse. Lucas was married to Maureen, who lived with him sometimes, when she wasn't teaching in Pennsylvania. He told Cybill that Maureen wasn't on Facebook, and Cybill wondered if Maureen had any idea he was such a Facebook slut.

The pretext was environmentalism. Two weeks after the conference, Lucas offered to drop off some signs and materials Cybill could use for her Expo, and she offered to make him some lunch. When he rang her bell, she saw that he was wearing not a warm, practical jacket such as most men their age wore in February, but a black and white tweed coat. In his long wool coat and long wool scarf, he looked at once old-fashioned and edgy. She hung up the coat, he kept the scarf draped around his neck, and they walked to the kitchen. While she was putting together sandwiches, he watched her every move. She was wearing her skinny gray jeans and her old red cowboy boots. She put down their plates and slid into a chair opposite him. He took a bite of the sandwich. In case he was a vegetarian, she had made sandwiches of fried mushrooms, roasted peppers, and mozzarella cheese. "Delicious," Lucas said. "Hostess, too." She shook her head and rolled her eyes upward, pleased nonetheless. "What, everybody tells you that?" asked Lucas.

That is what she came to like most about him: he demanded the meaning of every eye-roll, every slight frown, every small smile. He probed each hesitation and left absolutely nothing unsaid. This made her reckless in response, as she had never been so soon with a man. When he kissed her by the dishwasher, she kissed him back eagerly. It was a long and complex kiss that established their yearning and their expertise.

Soon, Cybill was up in Rain's room with him—for how could she bring Lucas to the room she shared with Quinn? Quinn was now in Montreal for a festival. On the twin bed beside Rain's china and glass horse collection, beneath posters for Seabiscuit and Los Lobos, Cybill discovered that Lucas could kiss for five minutes without stopping, and Lucas had a long vertical scar from open-heart surgery, and Lucas had strangely rough skin on his back and thighs.

She asked when they were resting, "Did you know it would be so good with us?" He nodded. "Since I first saw you across the auditorium. I thought, she's for me." This idea, that a mere glance in her direction had revealed her erotic capacity, excited Cybill so much she began caressing him again, with little thought to his damaged heart. He didn't seem to consider it either. Later, he said, "Not bad for an old guy."

"Don't say that!" she begged, as her breathing returned to normal.

He said, "Why not?"

"We're the same age, and I don't think of myself as 'an old gal.'"

He said, "You're much healthier than I am, and you look way younger. You're just gorgeous. Out of my league."

"We're the same league in bed," she observed.

He said, "That we are. You're perfect."

She said, "Don't get me started again," but it was too late, she had to give him a special kiss for saying that, and then he had to hold her breasts again. Soon, he whispered, "I think you need another." She was silent. He said, "You do, I can tell," so just like that he gave her one.

That night, as she was strolling down Facebook, she saw a post from Lucas: "inspirational afternoon. hoping to continue environmental synergy." Alone in her study, she felt her face redden: he was thanking her publicly for sleeping with him! And of course, his usual gaggle of Facebook friends had commented:

Margianna Davis: Intriguing, pls explain!

Josie Steinberg: Synergy is the most overused words of the decade.

Madeline White: The environment is an example of synergy!

Lucinda Porter: Still evangelical about global warming?

Lady Lacy: Or did you just have lunch with a new green babe?

The truth of this last was disturbing and exciting. A babe at her age! Lucas seemed to think so. Cybill saw that from now on, she would never be able to comment about any of his status reports. Now that they were secret lovers, she had to keep a low profile. Though she wanted to pounce all over his page, she could only prowl around; his name and hers could never be on the same thread. She continued traveling down the page, away from his postings and onto those of peripheral friends, when to her surprise, a box opened up on the lower right part of her screen.

She heard a small pop and saw the words "Chat: Lucas: hi."

Cybill was so startled she knocked the mouse off her desk. She noticed that under his words there was the image of a cloud with an arrow, the visual equivalent of quotation marks containing nothing. Near the image, a cursor blinked. She picked up the mouse from the floor, clicked and typed: "Lucas, are you there?" She wasn't sure how to send it, but she pressed "enter," heard that same small pop, and her words moved up the screen.

He wrote back, "no, i'm not." She was flooded with happiness or lust, she wasn't sure which, and wrote "Are we instant messaging?"

"yes. or chatting."

"Why don't you just call me up?"

"i can't. maureen will hear. this is more discreet."

"I've never done this before!"

"i won't hurt you, I promise," wrote Lucas, and Cybill was just grinning into the monitor, this was fun, a new way of communicating: semi-permanent.

She wrote, "Say something about me."

He wrote, "your kisses are amazing."

When they finally typed goodnight, she copied their dialogue and pasted it into a Word document so she could analyze it at length and see whether she had been too needy, too revealing, too suggestive. You couldn't do that with a telephone call.

They usually met at a cheap motel. It was better in a bigger bed, and they could move with abandon. Lucas sometimes gave a little grunting chuckle at Cybill's excitement, which only inflamed her further, and she whimpered and sighed in his arms. He was very gallant in bed, always insisting that she have one more than he did. This was obviously a source of pride, so she indulged him. Then he would leave, in his long tweed coat and long wool scarf.

Days would go by with no phone calls, no emails, no plans: only his maddening presence online—and the women who commented every time he rubbed his Facebook chin, or so it seemed to Cybill. He posted several times a day, always eliciting a female chorus of comments. He changed his profile picture almost daily, as if he were a girl of twenty privileging her friends with new aspects of her beauty. But he was a rumpled man in late middle age, and Cybill marveled at his vanity. She liked best the photograph where his head and eyes were tilted to one side, and his lips were smiling but closed (over those crooked teeth). But two days later it was replaced with a picture in which his eyes were altogether closed and there was a roll of flesh under his chin. The fact that he wasn't good-looking somehow made Cybill's obsession with him even worse.

She herself had used the same sunny, smiling Facebook profile picture for seven months. "Do you like it?" she asked Lucas when they were chatting on Facebook one night.

"it's too suburban mom," he replied.

When Jesse came home that weekend, Cybill got him to take some new pictures. He posed Cybill against a stone bridge in the late afternoon and took a dozen shots. In the one Cybill uploaded to Facebook, she was looking into the camera with her short blond hair blowing to one side. The golden light made her face radiant.

That night, Lucas im'd on Facebook: "it's great, it's so you. you're gorgeous—out of my league."

She had decided early on that chat with Lucas would always be uncensored, she'd type fast whatever she first thought, so she replied, her fingers reckless on the keys, "If I'm out of your league, why am I under your thumb?" He wrote back, in his usual lower case, "that's not true," but she felt it was. He was at the center of her thoughts, but she was not at the center of his; he had Maureen and his Facebook claque and who knew what or who else. Lucas added suddenly, "neither part actually," which wasn't fair, she thought, for he was the one who had used the phrase "out of my league." Twice.

One night while they were chatting on Facebook, Lucas asked if she wanted to play Scrabble. Cybill liked the game but didn't think virtual Scrabble would be any fun. She would have wanted to play holding Lucas's arm and watching his expression turn to alarm when she laid down seven tiles. In the actual world, they had never spent enough time together for board games, but now, thirty miles apart at midnight, she saw that playing Scrabble online might be another way of connecting, so Cybill said yes. Soon it became clear that Lucas was the superior player, making two and three and sometimes even four words a turn. When she remembered to look at the two-letter word list Facebook Scrabble obligingly provided, she began getting good scores herself, but then he made a seven-letter word (a "bingo" with a 50-point bonus) and she could never get close to him after that. This was a great relief, even a turn-on, to Cybill. She hated losing games to women, but she didn't mind losing to men. Indeed, she preferred it that way.

Lucas beat her by 85 points, and she felt her desire for him surge. "When can we see each other?" she asked on Facebook Scrabble chat.

He wrote, "come visit me at 10 on tuesday morning." This meant Maureen would be away and he was doing something else, probably environmental, on Tuesday afternoon.

It was four days until Tuesday, then it was three, and then it was two and Cybill awoke thinking tomorrow I'll be only one day away, and then it was tomorrow, and then it was 7:30 on the morning itself. And it was snowing hard: sheets of white whirled down outside the kitchen window. No cars moved; those parked by the curb were becoming white humps. Snow was predicted for the next four hours. No matter her yearning, she couldn't drive to his place in weather like this. She picked up the phone . . . then paused. Maybe Maureen hadn't left yet. Lucas wasn't on Facebook, for a change, so she sent him an email: So disappointed—can't venture out in this snow—let's reschedule soon. Call me, darling.

She loved calling him "darling," for it led him to call her "darling," and when he did so, even in chat or an email, she always felt loved and aroused. She thought that for a smart person she was not at all complex. This was a new thought of hers: that intelligent people could be simple. Cybill was eager to share this insight with Lucas. She waited in her kitchen while the snow fell outside. He didn't call. She called his cell at ten, but he didn't answer, so she left a message. She called again at eleven but this time didn't leave any message. Her number would be message enough. She saw he was now online on Facebook—just doodling around on Facebook! She sent him an instant message and he did not respond. Maybe he had left the room or maybe he was ignoring her. She "erased chat history" and logged off

Facebook so she wouldn't know either way. At eleven-thirty, the snow began to ease, and by noon, the sun was shining on a world of white. The snowplow arrived, and soon after that, cars began moving on the street.

She thought of Lucas's wide hands, like paws, pressed against her breasts. She thought of looking down at their conjoined bodies, abstract and bilaterally symmetrical, like a Rorschach image. She thought of his face as he moved above her and how though she usually closed her eyes while making love, with Lucas she opened them just before she came so his tender gaze could be part of it.

The next day he wrote her an email:
quite a storm. a big two inches fell. guess it was too much for you.

Cybill was outraged. It had been more than five inches in her town, and who was he, anyway, to demand that she travel in a snowstorm? Quinn would never ask her to do anything risky: concern for her well-being was one of his guiding principles. Sex wasn't everything, Cybill decided: Lucas had character flaws. She didn't write back and she didn't go on Facebook.

Two days later, she got another email from him. It said only:
uh-oh. now she's mad at me.

This didn't seem worth answering, either. His next Facebook status report bore the lament, "nobody loves me anymore." Naturally, his Facebook gaggle chimed in to deny this:

Lady Lacy: I still love you, Lucas!

Margianna Davis: Ah, baby, what's happening?

Madeline White: I'll be in your area Monday evening. Meet for a drink?

But Cybill held steady and ignored him. When the telephone rang, she looked at caller ID and did not pick up if it was Lucas. He left no messages on voicemail but finally wrote: listen, i'm sorry. i really am. please respond! your silence is driving me crazy! Driving him crazy was exactly the point, so Cybill decided to wait another few days.

But he drove to her house the next morning, and she let him in, and he was all over her, more intense and impassioned than he had ever been, except for the first time, perhaps. When Cybill got her usual bonus, it was hard to remember his character flaws. Afterwards, she cooked him a steak, for he wasn't a vegetarian after all. She loved watching him eat. In her current state, she felt she could happily watch Lucas doing anything at all: reading, washing the dishes, posting to his lady-friends on Facebook. They no longer mattered to Cybill, for she was getting him in the real world, and they were only reaching him in cyberspace. Probably.

Facebook Scrabble the next night was all about sex. They made the words GRAPPLE and ROMP and BLISS and HARDER and JISM, a word Cybill was surprised the Facebook Scrabble dictionary allowed. She got 32 points for it, at the end of the game, and ended up beating Lucas for the first time ever. She hoped it wouldn't alter their relationship.

The next day he put up a new profile picture of himself, with an eye-patch over one eye. He wrote: "i got my new ipad."

Madeline White: "How do you like it?"

Lucas: "i'm not sure what the point is. now i can't see out of that eye."

Cybill laughed aloud and found herself typing a response, but she did not send it, of course.

When she thought about Lucas, she used neutral terms like "intensity" so as not to use words like "joy." She told herself she was "fond of," rather than "mad for," him. She told herself she "didn't mind" about Maureen. Cybill even told herself that Lucas loved her: she could tell by the look in his eyes.

It snowed hard the day of their next rendezvous, at her house, and Cybill knew that Lucas would not postpone his visit. He was just childish enough to drive through a blizzard to demonstrate his devotion to her—and to show her up for not risking as much for him. She started calling his cell when he was half an hour late, but she never reached him, and he didn't call her. Finally, she called his landline and left an impersonal message on what she assumed was the general answering machine at his house, about urgently needing insurance for an environmental demonstration.

Three hours later, Cybill got a call. "Hi, my name is Maureen, and I'm married to Lucas. You left a message on our answering machine about demonstration insurance?"

Cybill sank to the couch and gasped. "Yes?"

"It sounded important, so I thought I'd call you back to say Lucas won't be able to help you with that. He had a heart attack today and he's in Memorial Hospital."

Cybill whispered, "Is he okay?"

"The doctors say he he's going to be fine."

"How did it happen?"

"He was shoveling snow in the driveway and he just collapsed. Luckily, I hadn't left yet, so we got to the hospital quickly."

The next afternoon, Cybill sat by his bedside at the hospital. Lucas looked terrible: tired, white, diminished. She said, "I did this to you. You were determined to dig your car out and see me. You had to prove a point, right?"

"Maybe I just wanted to see you."

She asked, "How bad is your heart? Should we stop seeing each other for now?" Lucas said nothing at all for a while, merely looked unhappy. "I'm not supposed to get excited," he said at last.

Cybill said, "I guess that answers my question. Oh, darling!"

"Darling," said Lucas. She felt the familiar sexual surge the word always brought when it came from Lucas, even a white, weakened Lucas, breaking up with her from a hospital bed. He said, "It might have been much worse."

This was true. He could have had an attack, or even died, while naked in her arms. Cybill said, "We could meet in restaurants, bars, public places," but Lucas wasn't interested in that.

Finally, he said, "You'd better go. Maureen's coming at four." Cybill left but lingered in the patients' lounge so she could catch a glimpse of Maureen. Lucas had described her as a blond fifteen years younger than himself, and a woman who fit that description walked briskly past the lounge and into Lucas's room. She was carrying flowers and carrier bags, and she exuded competence. She asked, "Honey, are you feeling any better?" Cybill did not hear his response but told herself she was glad Maureen was capable and caring.

For three weeks, as the event approached, the Green Expo occupied most of Cybill's waking moments. Would it all work out? Would the high school annex prove to be too small or too big? Would they have enough exhibitors and attendees to do it again the following year?

Then it was over. It had been a great success, and now she was writing a report about it to get additional funding the following year.

Late at night, after Quinn was asleep, she began logging onto Facebook again. Now that they were no longer lovers, she felt free to comment on Lucas's posts. Sometimes his ladyfriends commented on her comments. She became Facebook friends with two of them. The weeks wore on, and Lucas never suggested meeting Cybill. Without the prospect of an actual encounter, Cybill found his Facebook presence less urgent, his Facebook jokes less hilarious. She would observe he was online without necessarily chatting with him. She no longer answered his emails the hour or even the day she received them, although she continued to play Facebook Scrabble with him now and then.

Four months after the Green Expo, Cybill was still in touch with Lucas. Late at night, while Quinn was sleeping soundly in their bed, Cybill would tiptoe into her study and find Lucas and his girls on Facebook. And it wasn't really cheating, was it, to comment on a post of his? To open up the chat box and talk about her day? To banter and tease playing Scrabble, making the words MOUNT and THIGH and BITE?

Then Lucas made the word DARLING, a bingo.

When Cybill saw DARLING on the electronic Scrabble board and saw all the points he had made, she felt a rush of desire for him, despite Quinn in the very next room. Lucas now asked in chat, "What are you wearing?" She told him, and he pressed for more detail, which she provided. He told her what he missed most about her, and she replied "I miss your kisses."

"Ah, baby," he wrote, and so on and so forth. She knew it was all very trite, but it was also intensely absorbing. Facebook, which had shaped their affair from the start, was presenting them with a new opportunity via Scrabble chat. She asked whether he was excited, and he said he was. She was, too, she typed. And in this way, by mutual consent, Lucas, forbidden to her in the flesh, now became her Facebook lover.

10. McHUGH

2010

A couple of times a year, Cybill let McHugh take her to lunch. This had been going on for decades: they had met in graduate school, and now she was almost eligible to get social security. Although their meetings were rare, they persisted, and he had become one of her oldest friends, in both senses of old. He was ten years older than she, which was quite important when they were at Yale, then of no consequence for many years, and significant again now McHugh was in his seventies and shuffled, while Cybill still had a spring in her step.

Even when he was thirty-one, he had seemed elderly to her, which was why she always thought of him as McHugh and never as Tim. He approached her one day after class to comment on her Keats essay, and as their conversation continued, he suggested coffee. She was flattered by his interest in her paper. Soon, they began to talk about themselves. McHugh was married, with four children, and he taught two classes at New Haven University. Cybill was single, coasting on a fellowship that exempted her from teaching, and living on her own for the first time in her life. She was so free; he, so constrained. This was also true about their credos, Cybill thought, for he was a practicing Catholic and she was a practicing hippie, at least on weekends.

Looking back, Cybill was always grateful she had been single during that brief time, after the pill and before herpes or AIDS, when free love was in vogue. She had several, sometimes overlapping, lovers at Yale: a philosophy student, a musician, a

French instructor, and a handsome uncouth radical who picked his nose publicly. McHugh was not even a candidate. She never thought of him that way; indeed, she scarcely thought of him at all and was always mildly surprised to see him lurking by the door after their weekly seminar to ask her to elaborate on something she'd said in class.

One warm afternoon in May, Cybill sat on a Mexican blanket in a quad, enjoying the sun with Doug, the handsome radical. Their faces felt rubbery; their minds were streaming; they had taken mescaline two hours earlier. The grass was thick and green, and Cybill had taken off her sandals and was wriggling her toes in the "water" surrounding their "raft." She put her hand over Doug's. He looked down, and she did, too, and they both watched how her hand swelled and shriveled with her pulse. He pulled his hand out from under hers, shook it out, and stood up. "Are you all right?" she asked.

"Sure," he said, "but I have to go."

"Why?" she asked, but he just walked away. Had her pulsating hand repelled him? Her own muscles were like jelly; she couldn't have moved. She closed her eyes and began traveling down a tunnel she knew well from a recurrent dream, but since she was awake, she changed the outcome, and instead of arriving in a municipal office where they were counting ballots, she was on top of a mountain, looking across a wide valley to another mountain.

"Cybill?" A voice shook her out of her reverie. It was McHugh. The drug had provided her with a fish-eye lens, and with his big eyes and skinny limbs, McHugh resembled a bug. He chirped, "Can I join you?" Without waiting for an answer (she would have said No, for McHugh was not a person she wanted to talk to while tripping), he sat down beside her. He was wearing a button-down shirt and a sports coat; she was wearing a gauzy white Indian shirt and denim cut-offs. He said, "I've been thinking a lot about what you said about Byron."

Byron, Byron: what *had* she said about Byron? She said, "Let's talk about something else."

He said, "All right. Are you in love?"

"That's quite a jump," she said and thought, *uh-oh*. Now as well as hiding her high, she had to turn the conversation away from intimacy. She did not want to get close to McHugh, but he insisted.

"Are you?"

"Not in Byron's way," and she quoted, "'Man's love is of man's life a thing apart, 'Tis woman's whole existence.' No one is my whole existence, but I'm seeing someone." Actually, a couple of people, but he didn't have to know that. She asked, "Why, are you in love?"

"Oh, it's different when you're married," said McHugh. She did not ask him to explain but looked at the sky, which had amoeboid shapes in it, like paisley. Wasn't it just possible that they were always present and that the mescaline did not create them but rather allowed her to see them?

After a while McHugh said, "I'd better be off." He added, "Your pupils are enormous."

"Oh, that," she said. "I've just had an eye exam." She couldn't tell if he believed her.

He got his doctorate a year before she did and became an Assistant Professor at New Haven University. She moved to New York and married James. There were no college teaching jobs in New York, so her Ph.D. was ornamental rather than practical. She now saw that McHugh had been smart to establish himself at a university before getting his degree, and she wished she had done the same. Since she couldn't teach full-time, and teaching part-time as an adjunct made no sense financially, she took a few courses in advertising and landed a job as a copywriter. In a letter, McHugh deplored this waste of her "very fine mind," but Cybill rather enjoyed her job. He wrote her every few months, and her heart sank when she saw one of his envelopes in her mailbox, for it meant she would have to answer it. They had never been close; they weren't even old friends; why did he want to thicken their tie?

Once or twice a year, McHugh would say he would be in New

York on such and such a day, and could he take her to lunch? She wasn't sure if he really had business in New York or if he just came to see her, but she usually agreed. He reminded her that she might have been a scholar and a teacher.

Their lives were always out of synch. Cybill had her first baby, Rain, when McHugh's youngest child was leaving for college. She quit her job to be with the baby and worked freelance for the agency from home. One spring afternoon, McHugh dropped by for a visit. He admired Rain and held her easily while Cybill put on the kettle for their tea. He told her about his English department, where, to his dismay, structuralism was taking hold, and the students read more books about critical theory than they read actual novels or poems. She said, "I would have hated that. Perhaps it's for the best that I didn't end up in a college English department."

"No, no," said McHugh. "Don't say that. It's a crying shame that someone like you isn't inspiring young people to appreciate literature." Rain began to fuss, pulling at her ears.

"Is she hungry?" asked McHugh. "Are you nursing her?"

She thought she saw hope in his eye. "Not any more," said Cybill. "I think she's ready for her nap." She carried Rain to her crib and gave her the pacifier. Suck, suck, suck. Back in the living room, she joined McHugh on the couch.

"Cybill," he began, and then he leaned toward her and put his mouth on hers. Well! This simply won't do, she thought, I'm not attracted to him and never have been. But to her surprise, his thin lips felt quite pleasant. She would let McHugh kiss her a little longer, she decided, to reward him for his long devotion. Somehow, soon they were lying on the couch, and his hand passed over her blouse. We have to stop this, she thought, but then she was riding a warm wave and decided she would stay on it just a bit longer. Meanwhile, he was moving his body against hers and—oh, this was terrible!—she surged ecstatically and collapsed. He stopped moving, too, and was catching his breath. They hadn't opened a button nor moved a zipper. She would pretend nothing had happened, which was what he seemed to be doing as well.

She gave a strange little laugh and stood up. "Tim," she said. "You're a married man."

He said, "I'm getting a divorce. I was going to tell you."

"Well, I'm a married woman."

He said, "I thought perhaps you had an open marriage."

"Not at all!" She said, "Shall I get you another cup of tea and send you on your way?"

＊ ＊ ＊

In the years and decades to come, Cybill was profoundly grateful that he never mentioned what she thought of as The Episode, not naming it more specifically even in her mind. Sometimes she thought that McHugh's not mentioning it was what she liked most about him. She couldn't say why she was so ashamed of The Episode, but at least he didn't embarrass her by ever referring to their sole embrace, which had gotten so quickly and mysteriously out of hand.

Soon, along with his letters, he began sending her his poems. She would read these dutifully and try to find something intelligent and complimentary to say about them, but she found them hard going. She didn't read poetry much any more, so she was probably not a good judge. Once Jesse was born, Cybill was busy, and when she opened a book, it had to be a novel. McHugh occasionally got his poems published in literary magazines, so maybe they were okay after all.

When she turned forty-eight, Cybill fell into a funk. Replying to a letter from McHugh, she wrote, "My moods vary so much. Last month I felt I could do anything, but today I feel utterly insignificant and ineffectual." He wrote back, "Perhaps you're bipolar. Have you ever thought about taking lithium?" Cybill stared at the page. How could someone who'd known her so long understand her so little? They had nothing in common, nothing! What was the point in even corresponding?

But silence would not stop McHugh: he simply wrote another

letter. He had taken up running, and he and his daughters trained together. He had been promoted to full professor. He enclosed six more poems. At least none of them was about her, as far as she could tell.

After fifteen years as a single man, McHugh married a New York lawyer named Sally. Cybill felt she should have been invited to the wedding: after all, they had been friends for so long. But would she have invited him to a wedding with Quinn? Probably not.

"If you're so happy with Quinn why don't you marry him?" asked Johanna.

"Maybe I don't want to rock the boat. And also. He's never asked."

"He's probably waiting for you to ask."

"Perhaps you're right. But it doesn't matter one way or another to me."

"Perhaps you don't want to get married because you want a little, um, wiggle-room."

"What do you mean?"

"Well, Lucas and so on."

"No, I don't think so. It wouldn't make a difference. And Lucas was probably the last."

"Ha!" said Johanna.

After his marriage to Sally, McHugh spent half his time at his cottage on the shore near New Haven and half his time in Sally's Chelsea duplex. Though now he lived much closer to Cybill, their twice a year lunch schedule persisted. She wondered if he ever thought about The Episode. He published many scholarly articles and a popular textbook; she lost her major client, her old agency, when it went out of business. McHugh's career kept advancing; Cybill's declined. It was hard to find freelance assignments, and she spent as much time looking for work as actually working. During an especially dry spell, McHugh told her about his university's pension plan. By the time he left teaching, he'd have almost two million dollars in his retirement account. She stared at him across her quesadilla. Rain and Jesse had both chosen private colleges, and Cybill and James were in debt. That's why she had taken what she had characterized to Johanna as "this dumb marketing job," which came with grueling business travel. So she couldn't help resenting McHugh, who had done so well in academia, while she hadn't climbed the first rung. Yet in graduate school, she'd been considered brilliant, especially by McHugh. Now McHugh claimed that Harold Bloom liked his poems. Harold Bloom!

Cybill almost never wrote poetry herself, except when she was wracked by love. She never considered leaving Quinn, whom she felt she loved deeply. She felt she had affairs more for the joy (and the pain) than the sex. She was, she knew, an intensity junkie, and once in a while, she needed a dose.

Now she was in the middle of her affair with Lucas. She was glad he was married, as she had learned that partner symmetry worked best for affairs, but she wished he saw her more often and allowed himself more emotion. He seemed to see her mainly for sex, for he maintained that he and his Maureen never made love any more. Why not, she wondered, when he had all that natural talent? He told her she had talent, too, and praised her, rather rudely, which she didn't mind. She knew that being considered a sex object at her age was something of a triumph, but six months into the affair, emotionally aflame, what she wanted most from Lucas was the traditional three-word declaration. Since he wouldn't say it, she couldn't either. So she wrote a poem and called it "The Word." She read it to Lucas one afternoon while their coffee was dripping into a filter. "Very nice," he said, denying her what she wanted and pulling her shirt from her jeans so he could get at her skin. After that, she carried the poem in her handbag, so she could look at it anywhere and suffer.

McHugh continued to send his poems, now by email, to Cybill, and she was able to sincerely praise a heartfelt sequence about his mother's dementia. Two of these poems were accepted by *Ploughshares*. McHugh took her to lunch in the Village to celebrate. "Those are the first of my poems you've ever really liked," he marveled. "You have such a good eye."

"I sometimes write poems myself," Cybill admitted.

McHugh said, "I'd love to read them."

She said, impulsively, "I have one with me right now. It's called 'The Word.'" She handed him a paper folded in quarters. It had been folded and unfolded many times before. McHugh opened it and read:

> After all
> It's only a word
> A few letters
> A single syllable
>
> Not a needle to puncture our balloons
> Not an animal to ravish and ravage us
> Not a grenade to explode our two worlds
> And leave us crawling through the rubble
> To each other
>
> I'm almost sure of this
>
> We could tell the truth
> We could say the word
>
> You go first

McHugh looked up from the poem, his eyes wide with rapture. He said, "*I'll* go first! I love you, Cybill, I fell in love with you at Yale and I'll always love you!"

She cried, half standing, "No, no, Tim, stop, it's just a poem, and it's not about you."

"It's not about me?"

She sat down again. "I'm so sorry."

"Who is it about?"

She said, "No one. Everyone. Whoever wants to hear 'I love you.'"

McHugh said, "Poems don't usually come from an abstract

impulse like that. You were writing this to somebody, somebody married. That's why the word 'love' could explode the two worlds."

"Perhaps," said Cybill, snatching back her poem and folding it up. McHugh's eyes began to glisten and she had to look away. She said, "My fault. I'm really sorry, Tim."

Why had she shown him that poem? Because on some level she wanted to punish him for his success and her obscurity? Because of the money in his pension plan? Because she wanted to torment him by suggesting she was having an affair? She had never suspected McHugh would think the poem was about him. She had hoped he would talk about the metaphors or the line-breaks. *He* had hoped, she supposed, that they would declare themselves to each other at last. This was terrible: to have brought him so high and so low, so fast. The man across the table was wrinkled and old. He had seven grandchildren and a bum knee, and now a tear was running down his cheek. Cybill stood up and said, "I'm going to the ladies."

The walls of the bathroom were blue, and there was an overhead lamp fixture. Cybill's face was full of shadows, and she looked her age. Surely this thing with Lucas would be her last affair. But what about McHugh? What consolation could she offer for misleading him like this? And then, with horror, Cybill knew. It would be distasteful, but it was the only way. Surely she owed this to McHugh, whose admiration, no, love, had lasted so many years; McHugh who had laid himself raw; McHugh, whom she would never love back. She put her lipstick back in her handbag, walked to the table, and sat down.

He would not look at her, so she began to talk. "Tim, do you remember the time we got a little . . . physical?"

Then he did meet her eyes and said, "We kissed on your couch, of course I remember." Was he blushing?

She felt her own face redden as she recalled The Episode. She said, "Just a few kisses, right?"

He nodded and said, "That was thirty-two years ago."

Trust McHugh to remember exactly! Cybill said, "It's not

going to happen again."

"You've made that clear."

"Yes, but . . . you may be pleased to know . . ." Oh, God, how to phrase it?

"What?"

Cybill said, "Well, I've never had such a, um . . . *rapid* . . . experience in my life."

"Rapid?" He seemed puzzled. Then McHugh began to smile and said, "You, too?"

She nodded. "Can we never, ever mention this again?" Cybill begged. "Will you promise?"

"Okay," McHugh said, with an enormous grin. He really did look like a bug, a grasshopper, all eyes and mouth.

"And stop smiling smugly," said Cybill. This was as awful as she had imagined. She had to get out of there fast. "Waiter!" She held up her arm. "Could we have a check?"

Even after he paid, McHugh was still smiling, his wrinkles etched deep in his cheeks.

11. HER LAST AFFAIR

Given how they met, Cybill was always amused at the bookish nature of their affair. Jasper quoted poetry to her, and clipped out articles for her, and sat her down on a folding chair facing his so he could talk about the latest things he read. She loved looking at his face, his expressive brown eyes and elegant, downward-turning mouth, and was happy to sit opposite him with one of her bare feet tucked under his thigh as they discussed Barthes or Updike or David Foster Wallace. Hours might pass before Jasper would glance upward, toward the loft bed, and, feigning reluctance, Cybill would give a small nod. She always let him climb the ladder first. She did not want him below her, looking upwards at her thighs.

He said when they met that he lived in a "slot," and Cybill thought he was joking until she saw the place. It was a university dormitory room in midtown Manhattan, perhaps ten feet by ten feet, with a tiny bathroom attached. He had lived there for the past fifteen years. "Nothing extra," he said with satisfaction. No couch, no TV, no kitchen, no plants.

She admired his austerity. Still, it wasn't very comfortable at his place, and he would never come to hers because of Quinn. Even when Quinn was away in another state, Jasper refused to set foot in her house. "That shows how patriarchal you are," she said. "You think it's really his house."

"He could come home unexpectedly," Jasper said.

He wouldn't change his mind about this, so they always went to the slot. "Don't you want to picture me in my milieu?" she once asked.

"Yes." he said. "Show me photographs."

On their first date, they met for lunch at a restaurant. She was happy to recognize him, for it had been dark when they'd met at that somehow embarrassing event two weeks earlier. Now in daylight, she was relieved to find he was just as good-looking as she had remembered. But she was puzzled by his eating habits. "Order anything you like," he said, "but I'm not hungry." She ordered soup and a salad. He sipped a glass of water. They never stopped talking, interrupting each other in their need to express and respond and qualify. Afterwards, he paid for her meal and said, "Would you like to see my slot?"

She tried to conceal her surprise that a man of some talent and means, a lawyer and a Harvard graduate, lived so modestly. After all, what did she care? But she had to be careful in that loft bed: if she sat up abruptly, she would hit the ceiling with her head, and there was always the risk of tumbling down. And although sometimes that ceiling was useful (resting her feet on it provided good leverage), as the weeks continued, she wished that they could make love like ordinary people in late middle age, on a big, comfortable bed, listening to music from good speakers, setting down their wine glasses on night tables at each side of the bed before turning to each other anew.

My Last Affair was what she called this thing with Jasper. She termed it thus to herself and to Johanna, who, had seen her suffer and exult many times before. She said, "This isn't necessarily your last affair, you know."

"I'm sure it is," said Cybill.

Of course Jasper would be her last lover: how much longer could she keep carrying on like this, at her great age?

She did not want Jasper to find out how old she was, although he himself, at fifty-seven, was not exactly young. Cybill looked much younger than her years, but now that she was sixty-four, with Medicare only months away, she knew that her years of philandering were coming to an end. She was glad her last affair was with an attractive man who got so carried away when he spoke about books he sometimes stammered with excitement.

She would watch him talk, on his folding chair, and think how adorable he was, how well suited to be her last lover. After him, she would say goodbye to all that. Perhaps it was not too late to achieve durable success, besides having raised magnificent children. She felt her hectic romantic life had taken her best energies and suspected she would have achieved more worldly success had she ever renounced the emotional maelstrom.

❊ ❊ ❊

The oddest thing about her last affair was that she and Jasper had so little sexual chemistry. She was more aroused by the idea of him than by his physical touch. Early on, she dreamed of him and had an orgasm—or dreamed she did, for how could she tell the difference? Just the thought of him, while she was on her way to work or shopping for dinner, could make her swell and glow. But when Jasper actually touched her, there wasn't that thrill she expected to feel, given how much she liked looking at him. Even when they had just met and were lying on a mattress in the darkest part of the room, she had not felt excited when he clasped her hand—only astonished at how hard his palm felt against hers. They were side by side, facing the ceiling. She asked, "Do you do manual labor? Your hands are as hard as saddles." He said, "I do pull-ups."

The other odd thing about Jasper, besides the slot, and his diet, was that he always had at least two and usually three girlfriends concurrently. Cybill made four. "It works out better for me," Jasper said.

Cybill asked, "And for them?"

"They know it's my way," he replied.

Cybill knew she was in no position to object to Jasper's other girlfriends. After all, they all knew he was polyamorous, while she herself was living with Quinn and secretly seeing Jasper. Morally, she felt her own position was worse. Still, how did he manage to fit them all in?

Jasper emailed asking when she could meet him, at 2 or 2:30, and she replied only: "2 better, sooner." She hoped he might respond in kind, with something reckless and impetuous. She hoped he felt as hot reading those words as she did writing them. For passion and expression were always joined for her; she needed words to stoke the flames. But Jasper rarely added to the fire.

"Tell me about them," she asked. "Your other girlfriends." Cybill and Jasper were on the folding chairs drinking cheap wine. He drank his from a battered red plastic tumbler she tried to keep out of her line of vision. She drank hers from a squat glass with a thick lip.

He said, "Two of them are really ex-girlfriends I still see. The other one is newer."

She asked, "How do you have time for them all?"

He said, "It works out." Prodded, he told her that one had been a dancer and now ran a dance school. He saw her on Sundays, often with her grandchildren. Another was a Filipina doctor he had met as a patient. Some week nights she visited from New Jersey. The third was a lawyer who insisted on going to expensive restaurants and clubs. "And I have to pay," he told Cybill.

"She sounds awful."

Cybill and Jasper were just not sensually attuned. Sometimes when she stroked him, he would push her hand away and say, "That tickles." When she first moved down his body, he actually said, "You don't have to do that." He wasn't a very good lover and left her jangled and dissatisfied. She knew it was bizarre, and contrary to the usual dynamic, that she always came with her partner and never with her lover. Jasper didn't seem to notice anything was wrong and was surprised when she finally mentioned it.

❋ ❋ ❋

The next time she was up in his loft bed, Jasper added a new move to his routine, and after some of this, she gave a shout of pleasure. Jasper asked, politely, "Are you all right?" He seemed concerned.

"I'm fine!" she declared. She sat up to emphasize her well-being — and banged her head against the ceiling.

Didn't those other women make any sounds when they came? Or maybe they didn't come with him. In her experience, men as handsome as Jasper were usually not good lovers. They didn't have to be.

Oh, but he was charming! He always asked about her colleagues and her children, and if he sometimes asked the same question twice, surely he had a lot on his mind. Sometimes he complained about the third girlfriend, the lawyer, and Cybill always advised him to leave her. The fact that he put up with such a difficult woman signified that she was important to him. Cybill wanted to be the important woman in his life, but she made it all too easy, she knew. Whenever he wanted to see her, she always agreed. She had instantly gone to the mattress with him on the night that they met. They had started out by kissing, but soon they were on their backs, discussing the romantic poets.

Her friends knew Cybill had met Jasper at a party, but she'd never been more specific than that. It was the holiday party of a highbrow erotic website for which one of her friends blogged. Cybill pushed the door open and entered a large, dim room. Once her eyes got adjusted, she saw that there were drinks at one side of the room, dancing in the middle, and, in a corner, some mattresses on which people were cuddling. Her friend welcomed her at the door. Then she greeted a young woman wearing a bustier. Cybill found a drink and spoke to a cartoonist. Then she moved to the middle of the room, where she danced alone. A dark-haired man was watching her, and when the music paused he said, "You dance so well."

"Come join me," she said.

He said, "No, I don't dance." And now Jasper smiled. He said, "I thought we could lie down and talk."

* * *

"So how do you think of me?" she asked rashly one afternoon. They were racing through the streets of Greenwich Village to get to a lecture sponsored by PEN. Cybill went on: "There's the dancer and the doctor and the lawyer and . . . how do you think of me?" She wondered whether he would say the marketer or, and she hoped for this, the intellectual, because of their happiness skiing the cultural terrain. Jasper mumbled something. She couldn't believe what she'd heard and said, "What did you say?"

Then Jasper said clearly, "The soul mate." She stopped dead on the sidewalk, bolted to it by joy. He said, "Come on, we're late."

She put her finger to his lips and said, "No. Don't say another word." For Cybill wanted to stand in the golden bell jar of "soul mate" and breathe. It was for moments like this, and not sex, that she had love affairs, and she sensed that this was it, the high point of her last affair, so she was nostalgic for the moment even as it was occurring. Jasper pulled her arm, and she hurried with him over the cobblestones.

She thought of Jasper first thing in the morning and last thing before sleeping. This was her pattern: her current lover was always her obsession. She would compose teasing and revealing emails, most of which she never sent. She would create endless "what if?" scenarios. Much of what she saw and did would be magically connected to her lover, but only her three best friends could know this: never the lover himself. He already had too much power, which was how she liked it. Affairs brought her unbalance, disequilibrium, fear, joy. They made life more extreme.

"How was your panel?" Jasper asked. The red plastic tumbler was in his hand, the thick-lipped one in hers.

She said, "It was fine. We had a good turn-out, and the other panelists were good. One of them spoke about 'the forbidden' in marketing, and why we should go there. A new thought."

Jasper said, "Maybe we should go upstairs." He indicated the loft bed with his chin. Half an hour later, he asked, "How was your panel?"

Cybill asked Jasper theoretically (or perhaps "theoretically"), "Wouldn't you rather have a love affair than just an affair?"

He said, "I'd rather not have histrionics."

She celebrated her birthday with a dinner party, to which she invited her family and her closest friends. Sixty-five! She looked at the mirror for changes. Perhaps she should get some cosmetic filler for the lines by the corners of her mouth, but Quinn said she didn't need to do a thing. She didn't tell Jasper about her birthday dinner-party, in case he asked the question she didn't want to answer.

Once Jasper laughed when he came, and while she did not do either, Cybill found this so endearing she caressed his shoulder. He shook her hand off, saying, "That tickles."

When Jasper got a promotion at work, Cybill suggested that they celebrate. He agreed to a drink at a fancy hotel nearby, which had a dark lobby with provocative original art. Rooms started at $525 a night, so she knew that the drinks would also be pricy. Still, she was startled when Jasper ordered one of their special martinis to be split between the two of them. "To see if I like it," he told the waiter, but Cybill was shocked. Then he said, "Lift your hair up off your face," and she complied, and he said, "That looks beautiful. You should wear your hair up all the time." She was wearing her hair long that year. She rummaged in her bag for her tortoise-shell hair clip. With one hand, she brought her hair into a topknot; with the other hand, she clipped it. Jasper said, "Now I can look at your face, see your ears, watch your beautiful mouth." They finished the single cocktail and rushed back to his place.

He seemed to have forgotten the move that was so successful with her, and after they made love, she lay staring at the very close ceiling while he breathed deeply in sleep. As always when he slept after sex, he apologized when he awoke. "Sorry about that. It must have been the cocktail."

She said, "It was only half a cocktail."

Jasper said "I wish I didn't always fall sleep. It's not very polite."

"People aren't always polite about sex," she replied. She wanted to say, "If you were really polite, you would do what I liked in bed."

❄ ❄ ❄

Now Cybill always wore her hair up for Jasper, which meant she always wore earrings, which meant she always had to take them off before the ascent, which meant she made a little striptease of the process, looking into his eyes and slowly disengaging the wires, which meant she had to lay them down carefully so they wouldn't get lost. She let him undo the hairclip and run his fingers down her loose hair. And soon, this too became routine, and he moved his hands hurriedly through her hair.

Citing pressure at work, Jasper began spacing their dates more widely, once every ten days or two weeks, rather than weekly. And he stopped sending articles for her to read. She realized that her last affair was winding down. Jasper's emails, always formal, became even stiffer and less frequent. For months, she had warmed herself over "soul mate," but now even that was getting cold.

She didn't hear from him for three weeks. Finally, she wrote to him: "Hey, when are we getting together?" No histrionics. But he never wrote back. Cybill supposed he had met someone new, and five concurrent girlfriends was really too many. Still, he had been seeing her for nine months. Shouldn't he give her some explanation? Somehow, she couldn't bear to call him.

No Jasper. That's what she woke up thinking. No Jasper. I'm sixty-five years old and I've had my last affair. No more sweet anticipation. No more surge of joy at the sight of a face. No more turmoil. No Jasper. The area around her heart felt bruised, even though she had known for some time that they were incompatible. She began reconsidering Jasper, and now he no longer seemed eccentric — just stingy: with his money, with his body, with his heart.

12. BODYPAINT

2014

Surely there were other ways to get full-body excitement besides a new affair! There was hang-gliding, or free rock climbing, or kitesurfing on ice. Cybill knew these pursuits would be thrilling, but she had never been drawn to dangerous sports; she didn't even like watching them on TV.

Maybe there was something less risky she could do with Quinn. Tennis? Ping pong? Paddle ball? But Quinn was neither athletic nor competitive: he got his muscles via weights at the gym.

Swing dancing? Drum circles? Kayaking? She proposed each of these, over several weeks, and saw that Quinn would do them for her but without enthusiasm. Maybe she shouldn't let that stop her. After all, she had talked him into the bliss workshop (what, 14 years earlier?) and while initially dubious, he had enjoyed it in the end. And it really had brought them closer.

So she paused when she saw a listing in NextDoor:

> *Local artist expanding portfolio. Seeking models, aged 50+, for bodypainting in your home. Please visit my website: paintingonpeople.net.*

When Cybill opened the web page, she saw a single photograph of a woman, viewed from behind, her body painted in a colorful, sinuous grid. Cybill clicked on through a series of stunning images. The artist, whose name was Larry Zander, painted directly on nude people, using them as his canvas. The results were original and beautiful. When she came across a photo of two twenty-year-olds back-to-back with Zander's design binding them together, she thought it would be wonderful to do this with Quinn.

That night after dinner, she showed Quinn Zander's website and said, "What do you think?"

He responded as she suspected he would, with a bland, "Very nice."

"He's really good, don't you think?"

"Sure. I like the way he made this couple into one design. The way the lines connect them."

The perfect opening! Cybill said, "That could be us."

"What do you mean?"

"He's looking for older models. See?" And she showed him the NextDoor listing. "You just about qualify, youngster!"

"Yeah, but Cybill. That's really out there! Taking off our clothes and getting painted? Who is this guy? Some kind of perve?"

"Not at all. He's a serious artist. Look at his bio." And she clicked to show Quinn that Zander's work was in the permanent collection of museums in San Francisco and New York. "Maybe we could be on the wall of a museum! Wouldn't that be cool?"

"I don't know. I mean, *nude?*"

"Aren't you proud of that body of yours? Given the hours you lavish on it at the gym?"

"Well, yeah, but . . ."

"He's not going to display our genitals. See? He crops judiciously." She clicked through the photos again. It was true, and Cybill pressed her advantage. "Just look at these images. Do you find any of them sexually exciting?"

"No. Not at all."

"That's what I mean. This isn't porn. It's art! And we could *be* art." And now she removed the last arrow from her quiver. She said, "It would be a first for us."

"That's true." Long pause. "Well, all right, then. I guess."

"Oh, honey, that's so sweet of you." She scratched his head. "You'll see. It will be fun." He was silent with pleasure, or dismay—or, Cybill thought, maybe both.

Cybill arranged for Zander to come to the house the following Sunday. On Saturday, over bagels and lox, Quinn said, "I've been thinking. This bodypainting is more your thing than mine. Why not just let him paint you? I can hang out in the room as your chaperone."

Cybill said, "I don't need a chaperone." She turned away in silence.

"What?" asked Quinn.

"I'm so disappointed."

"Why?"

"I thought we would do this together as a sign of our love. Two bodies, one image. The two of us forever connected." As she spoke, she felt her eyes get wet.

"Oh, Cybill." He took her in his arms. "When you put it like that, of course I'll do it with you. But I can't help feeling nervous. What if one of my students sees it?"

"They'll admire the design and your daring, my darling."

"I guess."

"You'll see. It will be an adventure."

That night when she got up to pee, Quinn was gone from the bed, reading in the living room. "Honey," she called down. "It's three-thirty. Come back to bed."

"I can't sleep. I had a bad dream and woke up."

"What was the dream about?"

"That guy who's coming to paint us. He made us strip and go under a limbo stick."

"A limbo stick?" Cybill giggled. "Where does that come from?"

"I don't know," said Quinn. "I'll be there soon." But he stayed up another hour.

The next day at noon, Zander arrived with his drop cloths and paints. He was a man of early middle age with short brown hair and a gentle manner. Cybill and Quinn led him into her dining room, which had the best light in the house. "Thank you for letting me paint you both," Zander said. "I've painted hundreds of bodies, mainly at public events. But I've rarely painted anyone over 50. I feel it's a lack."

"I see you've painted disabled children," said Cybill, who had read this in Wikipedia.

"That was so much fun," said Zander. "But they're kids, they get impatient. I had to paint very quickly."

"How long will it take today?"

"A couple of hours."

"A couple of *hours?*" asked Quinn.

Zander said, "I'll give you a break in the middle. And you'll be in a comfortable position."

"That's fine," said Cybill, giving Quinn a look. "I feel so lucky you're here," she told Zander. "Your work is so beautiful."

"Thank you."

"But so temporary," said Quinn. "I mean, won't we need to shower off the paint?"

"Not before I document you," said Zander. He gestured toward his camera. "Speaking of which, could you sign these releases?"

"How will you use the photographs?" asked Quinn, pen in hand.

"I don't know. Maybe not at all. Maybe in an exhibition. Or maybe on my website. I'll send you the best of the bunch."

This seemed to Cybill a great bargain: a couple of hours in exchange for a permanent image of their love. Cybill and Quinn signed the documents and went upstairs to take off their clothes.

"Are you okay?" asked Cybill.

"I guess," said Quinn. They put on robes over their naked bodies, although the house was very warm and they would take off the robes as soon as they were downstairs. When they got to the first floor, they saw that Zander had moved a small couch from the living room into the dining room and laid a beige canvas drop cloth upon it. He said, "Why don't you get comfortable on that?"

Cybill and Quinn took off their robes, and there they were,

revealed in their winter whiteness. Once again, Cybill worried about her unequal breasts, but Zander was mixing his colors and did not look up. She sat down awkwardly on the couch and leaned back against the armrest. Quinn lay down against her, more or less hiding her C and D breasts. His body was smooth and hairless, without an extra ounce—a perfect canvas, she thought. She wasn't so sure about her own body. At sixty-six, she had some sags and some cellulite, usually hidden by her clothes. But Quinn was covering most of her now, his back against her belly, and she began to relax. After all, Zander had specifically called for older bodies. They, too—*we*, too, she corrected herself—could provide inspiration and beauty.

The artist looked at them from many angles, including from up on a stool. He adjusted one of Quinn's legs and one of Cybill's arms. At last, he was satisfied with their joint position. Then he daubed bright pink onto his brush and began to paint. When the brush touched her skin, it was so light she could scarcely feel it. She couldn't tell what shapes he was painting, but now Zander was moving quickly from one of them to the other and then to his paints. He applied yellow and green to their skin, quickly and silently dabbing here and there. He was in the zone. Good for him!

But Cybill was worried about Quinn. She had talked him into getting his body painted, and he'd had nightmares about it. Because he was lying upon her, she couldn't see his face. She hoped he wasn't uptight and self-conscious. He was, after all, both more conservative and more exposed than she was. Cybill hoped he wasn't resenting her thirst for excitement and where it had taken them now.

But Quinn seemed relaxed against her, and his breath was steady. "Quinn," she whispered. "Are you okay?"

There was no reply, just a little . . . was that a snore?

Zander smiled. "I wouldn't worry about him," he said. "The brush can be very hypnotic. He's so relaxed he's fallen fast asleep."

Incredibly, it was true. Quinn's head was heavy on her breast. But Cybill was awake and alert.

13. HERE COMES TROUBLE

2015

Holly, Cybill's London friend, called to say that her friend Ben was moving to America with his wife Lucy and that they had rented a house in the very suburb where Cybill lived with Quinn. Cybill's first thought was that maybe these Brits could be couple-friends for her and Quinn. Disinclined to pay high taxes for the excellent schools their families no longer needed, many of their friends moved away when their children graduated from high school. Cybill herself had no plans to sell, but in the last four years, she and Quinn had lost three couple-friends to less expensive counties and states. Ben and Lucy, Cybill thought, might expand their shrunken social circle, though Holly didn't seem to like Lucy as much as she liked Ben.

The couple was curiously elusive. Cybill exchanged a few short emails with Ben, finally asking them to dinner on a specific date the following week, but there was no response to this invitation. Finally, after the date, Ben wrote back, saying that they were away. His tone was not apologetic enough, Cybill felt. Maybe Lucy was nicer. And then Cybill forgot about them both,

A few weeks later, her phone chimed with a text from Ben. "My cleaning lady is kicking me out, and the library's still closed. Can I come over?"

"Give me 15 mins," she found herself texting back.

But why had she agreed? How entitled he was, assuming he could just come over and meet her on such little notice! And pretending not to know about the laptop-friendly cafes in the village where he could stay until the library opened. Yet Holly really liked him. She said, "He's smart and he's funny, and he's curious about everything."

Still, Cybill didn't bother changing out of her comfortable flannel shirt and old jeans. Nor did she put on lipstick. She supposed he would want coffee, and she was adding water to the machine when the doorbell rang. She opened the door, and he walked across the threshold.

She closed the front door behind him and led him to the kitchen. Ben was very tall with strong features and thin lips.

When he smiled down at her and said, "Hi," Cybill had one distinct, jubilant thought: Here comes trouble!

Why? She couldn't say, not then, not later, after he had left, and certainly not later still when she and Ben spoke about those initial moments with awe.

There they were, aflame, surrounded by an empty house with many bedrooms.

It had been several years since her thing with Jasper, and Cybill had finally admitted to herself (duh!) that she felt closer to Quinn when there was no other man in her life. Life was simpler and smoother loving just one man, and it was deeply right to focus on the person who cherished her most. In years past, Cybill had enjoyed her occasional philandering, but come on! All of that had surely come to an end.

Then Ben walked into her kitchen. He was not a handsome man, but he was sexy, a *jolie laide* as the French would say. As they talked, she felt oddly elated, or, rather, ignited. He wasn't British after all—he was an American who had lived in London for a dozen years; his wife, Lucy, was originally from Westchester, and upon his retirement from university teaching, she wanted to return to the area.

It turned out they had rented a house just two blocks from Cybill's.

Much too close.

Ben drank coffee and ate warm rolls with butter and jam and told her how he spent his time. He had joined a history writers' group and was volunteering with Meals on Wheels. He did the shopping and half of the cooking. Lucy, ten years younger than Cybill, was studying to get her New York State license to resume work as a physical therapist.

Cybill told Ben that Quinn had recently joined the staff of a private school across the county, teaching music to children.

That was why she was free and alone in the daytime, she did not say, but surely Ben could add two plus two. Or one plus one.

He finished his second cup of coffee, stood up, said goodbye, and left.

Cybill began to doubt that initial flash between them. Well, anyway, it was good to meet him at last, though it might not be great, after all, to be couple-friends—not while he excited her like this. She wasn't good about hiding her feelings.

Ben texted her the next morning, asking if she had any more of those wonderful rolls. Just seeing his name in the messaging app gave her the "funny feeling": excitement, fear; joy, doubt; oxytocin, adrenaline; heat in her chest, swelling below.

She changed into a form-fitting sweater. Ben was at her house minutes later. This time, their talk was more personal, their glances more direct. His eyes were large and green, not luminescent, but solid, like marble. But he left without touching her. As they parted, instead of kissing on the cheek, they bobbed their heads across three feet of space in the doorway.

The third time he came over, she told him to use the back entrance so he wouldn't be banging on her front door in full view of her neighbors, and this hiding of their non-affair was, she felt, itself provocative, although he didn't comment. They had their usual animated conversation and once again he left without touching her, as if he had never heard of the three-date rule. Of course, these weren't dates. And they both had spouses, or the equivalent. But why would he keep coming around if he wasn't interested in her? He just can't help himself, Cybill thought. He can't help himself any more than I can help myself throwing open the door and gazing up at him. (He was six-foot-five, she had learned.) We are fated.

Visit number four followed the pattern: all yearning and no action, although their conversation was increasingly intimate, even sexy. Somehow *(somehow!)* they got on the subject of sexual novelty. Ben said, "I have a friend who puts it this way. 'The new piece of ass is always better than the old piece of ass even when the old piece of ass is better than the new piece of ass.'"

"How elegantly expressed," Cybill said, rolling her eyes. She said, "There's this Nabokov book where the young hero is having an affair with a married woman, and they're making love three times a week and he's thinking how much more they would do it if he could only move in with her! But the author's clearly skeptical."

They smiled at each other. He had finished his second roll, and suddenly she couldn't stand their undefined relationship for one additional second! She touched his hand and said, "Today before you leave, maybe we should sit on the couch and make out a little bit."

He looked stunned, so she withdrew her hand and said quickly, softening the blow, "Just a little bit." She held up thumb and index in a humorous little pinch.

I've just thrown myself at him, she realized. It's come to that!

He was not responding well. "Well, I, uh . . ." He took out his phone and looked into it.

Cybill couldn't bear being in the same room as him. She had been turned down! Men get this all the time, she knew, but it hadn't happened very often in her life. And God, it was humiliating. She left the kitchen, found her own phone, and scrolled through her email.

He called out goodbye and left by the back door.

His text came two hours later. "Will I see you tomorrow?"

The five most beautiful words in the English language! But she wasn't going to get into the same situation as today. She would never be alone in the house with him until their relationship changed, for she would probably hurl herself at him again, and for whatever reason, he didn't want that.

But deep down, she was certain, he did!

"Let's get high and go out for breakfast," she texted back.

And Ben wrote back, "YES."

What were they, a couple of teenagers?

Oh, to be alive in this new world!

They chose a down-market breakfast chain in the next town to avoid meeting anyone she knew. He didn't know many local people, but she had lived here for decades, and while surely a man and a woman could have an innocent meal together, she felt breakfast with Ben, whether in her own kitchen or at iHOP, would never be innocent. She would always be plotting to pique his desire.

They got stoned in the parking lot to enhance the eating experience, and the pot seemed to crack Ben wide open. After they had given the waiter their order, he said to Cybill, "I have to tell you something."

"Go on."

"Meeting you has been the best thing about moving here."

Cybill almost swooned. But she merely said, "Yeah?"

"Oh, yeah. By far."

She said, "So what happened yesterday? Did I scare you? Did I misread your signals?"

"No. Well. Maybe. Yes. I mean, do you want to break up your marriage?"

"Ben!" She had to laugh. "I thought you were more sophisticated than that. London and a university career and all."

"I'm just a hick," he agreed.

She said, "You have to understand. I would never leave Quinn. We're not married, by the way, but we've been together for decades and we adore each other. But once in a while, I just get a *feeling* for somebody else. It has nothing to do with me and Quinn."

"So, when did you last have this feeling?"

"Four years ago. I dubbed it 'my last affair.'"

"And now?"

"Well, Ben," she said, daring herself to continue and letting the weed sweep her past common sense. "We're already having an affair, and we haven't even touched."

"We have now," he said, putting his large, heavy hand over hers and resting it there, in full view of the world.

Rapture and terror.

Their pancakes arrived. He removed his hand from hers. They each made a show of putting on the soft butter and syrup, but neither could eat. They looked at each other and then looked away.

"A waste of good food," she said finally, loading up her fork and regarding the sticky, soggy mess it now held. She made herself put it into her mouth. She chewed and swallowed, and it was perfectly fine. "It's good, Ben," she said. "Try some."

"So, I was hoping," she said after a while, "that you and Lucy had an open marriage or something."

Ben shook his head. "Not at all. You and Quinn?"

She shook her head. "We've never actually talked about it, but I imagine the default for him is 'never,' and the default for me is 'when I just can't resist.'"

He put his hand over hers again. "Well," he said, "this is all good to know. I'm crazy about you. You know that, right?"

"I kind of do. And I like you, too," she said, surely the understatement of the year. "But I don't want you to risk things with Lucy."

He squeezed her hand. "Don't worry about that. But there is something else."

"Besides the fact that we're neighbors and your wife or my partner might find out? And that our every text and visit carries risk? And that we must never, ever tell Holly?"

He smiled. "Yeah, besides all that."

"So . . . what is it?"

He said, "Hasn't this been a beautiful morning?"

She nodded.

"So, I'll tell you later. Next time."

"When will that be?" She was suddenly anxious. It was Friday, and the weekend loomed ahead.

"Monday," he said.

He called for the check. Their plates were empty; they had managed to eat their pancakes after all.

On Sunday, he texted her:

> Maybe you need something at the supermarket and you can run into a friend there.

RUSH! It was a full-body experience, like being dipped in warm butterscotch sauce. He could do this to her with a simple text.
I love the thought, she wrote, but no.

Later, she texted him:

> Who is more smitten, he who needs to see her face or she who knows she can't see his without kissing it?

He wrote back:

> I was smitten the moment I saw you.

"Smitten"! So *that* was their word. Perhaps he would kiss her the next time he came around.

She deleted their texts, as she always did, sad to erase their ardent exchanges. But when she thought the word "smitten," she got the funny feeling all over again, and Cybill had the strange thought that perhaps her crush on Ben was more about getting her to a private ecstasy than about Ben himself. By now, in late middle age, she would have expected her feelings to be less extreme, but as far as she could recall, she had never been more euphoric and terrified than now. Sometimes when she thought about Ben, she could scarcely walk, scarcely breathe.

What was going on? Could she Google it? She typed "What happens to the body when we fall in love?" And soon she was reading the words of a neuroscientist named Stephanie Caciopoppo:

> *The first thing you'll notice if you've ever fallen in love is how good it feels. "Euphoria" is often the way we describe this state.*

Oh, yes, thought Cybill. How good it feels.

> *Falling in love sets off a whole array of biological fireworks...*
> *The brain is flooded by a joyous bath of dopamine. Your brain*
> *also increases the production of norepinephrine . . . skewering*
> *your perception of time. . . Physical contact triggers . . . ocytocin.*
> *. . that increases our feelings of empathy and trust.*

Who could ignore these biological fireworks? Not I! thought Cybill.

On Monday, Ben came into the house and brought her straight to the living room couch. And there they kissed and held each other: nothing more than that. But who would want anything more, when kissing him was like entering a warm, moonlit lake? Was it only her feeling for him (smitten!) that made their kissing rhapsodic? His mouth always knew what her mouth wanted most: lip, tongue; pressure, softness; dryness, wetness; rhythm, rest.

She pulled away to look into his eyes. "Wow."

He nodded.

She asked, "So what was that thing you were going to tell me?"

"Yes, we have to talk about that." They both straightened up on the couch. He reached for her hand. He said, "I have this medical condition."

"Heart?" she said, thinking of Lucas, her Facebook lover.

"It's not dangerous like that," Ben said. "And I'm perfectly healthy right now. But I had cancer a couple of years ago and they had to remove my prostate."

"Ah." What did that mean? It was some internal man thing, wasn't it? "Well, I'm glad you're healthy now."

"Yeah, but Cybill, it means I can't easily or maybe not at all . . . make love in the usual sense."

"That's okay," she said, and it was. "Just keep kissing me, sweetheart."

"We could do more than that," he said finally. "Let's find a bed."

She led him to the guest room with the double bed, and they

fell upon each other.

The next day, it occurred to Cybill that no one in the entire world except themselves would be happy that she and Ben were together. No one, certainly not Johanna or Holly, would say, "Congratulations! How glorious for you both!" Most people would be appalled—and mystified as well, considering she had Quinn.

But who cared about other people and their petty minds!

A week later, when she and Ben were in the guest bedroom, she shared some important news with him, news she could tell no one else. She said into his ear, "You realize what's going on here, don't you?"

"Mmmmh?"

She pulled away to look into his eyes. Thrillingly, dangerously, they were going over the precipice! She said to him, "We've fallen in love."

He tightened his hold on her and said, "Yes."

They did not talk about it again, but it was the foundation and justification for everything they did together. She knew she shouldn't see him most weekday mornings, but she always said yes when he asked.

Nothing is more beautiful than this, she thought, nothing!

And she knew he felt it too.

Not since she had first met Quinn had Cybill had such a mutual relationship. She had usually been the lover, the supplicant. But with Ben she was finding that passion was more powerful, more poignant, when it was returned. Just thinking about his feelings for her gave her that funny (and not funny) feeling, that hot body rush.

The next time that they were in bed, he said, "I'm worried that you'll break my heart."

Thrilled at this prospect, this power, she said, "I would never do that. Hurting you would be hurting myself."

It didn't seem to matter that they weren't exactly having sexual intercourse. (Cybill knew that if, God forbid, Quinn ever found out about her and Ben, this detail would provide consolation.)

To get an erection, he had to activate, through his scrotum, an internal pump which put fluid into his penis. "My little penis," he lamented. "It used to be so big." It wasn't quite firm enough to penetrate her, but he could come, or at least he claimed he could—without ejaculate. In a way, that was an advantage. The sheets in the guest bedroom always stayed fresh.

On Valentine's Day, he texted heart emojis and wrote: "You make me so happy. Your mind. Your warmth. Your coffee. Best of all, you let me take off your clothes, grab your hips, and smother your lips with mine."

Cybill memorized this, testing herself several times before deleting the message. Sometimes just before sleep she would play his Valentine text in her mind.

In his arms, she asked him once, "Who taught you how to kiss like this?"

And Ben said, "You did."

This exchange, too, she would often replay.

One morning, he did something extraordinary. He was on top of her, his hand between her legs, and she was almost there but worried she might lose her way. Then he suddenly bent his head down and kissed her right breast—sending Cybill to the moon.

She hoped he would repeat this some other time, but he didn't, although he did other nice things. She thought that maybe people simply forgot what they did while making love. Maybe that was why Jasper had never repeated his one great move.

One afternoon, three months after Ben and Cybill's blissful mornings began, Cybill heard a knock at her front door. She opened it to find a woman whom she didn't know. She was tall and thin with short black hair, beautiful blue eyes, and an angry expression. The woman said, "Hello. I'm Lucy. Ben's wife."

"Oh, God," said Cybill.

"Yeah, oh, God." They stared at each other. Lucy said, "Can I come in?"

Cybill held the door open.

Lucy came into the living room. "Nice house," she said. "So, this is where Ben spends every morning!"

"Not every morning," Cybill said faintly. "Does he know you're here?"

"No."

"So why *are* you here?"

"I'm here to say—you have to stop seeing my husband!"

"I don't know if I can do that," said Cybill.

Lucy said, "What do you mean?"

"What if we've fallen in love?"

"I don't give two shits about that!" shouted Lucy. "He's my husband, and I'll ruin your life if you see him again."

How would she know? What could she do?

As if reading her mind, Lucy said, "Oh, I'll know all right. All I have to do is go up to my attic window and I can see him going into your back door. He kept saying he was going to the library, but one day I decided to follow him."

She glared at Cybill. But there were tears in her eyes.

Cybill said, "He doesn't want to leave you. It's not like that."

"I don't care what it's like. You have to stop. Or I'll tell Quinn. And each of your children. Rain. And Jesse. And Frederick."

"Daniel," corrected Cybill automatically. "How do you know all this?"

Lucy just said, "Please. And there's social media. Facebook, Instagram—oh, and what about NextDoor?"

"You wouldn't do that," Cybill said.

"Try me."

Cybill said, "This has nothing to do with your marriage! I don't see why you're so upset."

"Of course you don't! You edited that horrible book about adultery! To you it's just love, romance and high-falutin emotion. But get real. People get jealous, people get hurt! Most people take their marriage vows seriously! Most people have a little self-restraint. I think your book and your ideas are completely disgusting."

"I guess you don't have much joy in your life," Cybill said, "and you don't want anyone else to have any either."

"Save your pity," said Lucy. "You're the old woman."

"That must really get you mad."

"It *is* a little weird, but no man ever leaves his wife for an older woman."

Cybill held back from saying Ben would.

Lucy said, "Do we have an agreement?"

Cybill said, "Can I see Ben to say goodbye?"

"Do it by text," Lucy said. And she quoted Cybill's last text, sneering: "See you Friday, my beloved." And with that, she turned and left the house.

Apparently, Ben was not as strict about deleting texts as she was.

They said goodbye by phone. Ben told Cybill that, yes, if they ever saw each other again, Lucy would do exactly as she'd threatened, and he was certain that she'd know. "She probably has a tracker on my phone."

"How can you love a woman like that?"

"I'm not sure I do." There was a small silence. Then he said, "But you would never leave Quinn."

She agreed. "I would never leave Quinn."

"You don't love me that much after all."

"That's not fair," she said. "You have no idea how I feel." There was a short silence. Then she said, "Don't let's quarrel now. It was thrilling being together!"

"It was," he said. "And you were always so kind about my …handicap."

"I didn't mind," she said. "It was rather endearing."

A few weeks later, Holly called from London to say that Ben and Lucy were buying the house they'd been renting.

Cybill thought: So, Ben will be here forever, two blocks away and untouchable!

And Lucy will always be able to see the back door of my house from her attic window. Ironic, Cybill thought, that she'd asked him to enter the house from the back.

Holly asked, "Whatever happened with you two? Didn't you like Ben?"

"Ben's great," Cybill said. "But Lucy and I don't get on. She seems very humorless. Conventional. I had hoped we might all be friends, but now I don't think so."

Holly said, "Yeah, Lucy can be a pill. But those gorgeous blue eyes!"

The first weeks she and Ben were apart, Cybill was tortured, knowing she might see him at the library, the post office, or Starbuck's. What would she do? Run into his arms—or bolt in the other direction? But months went by, and she and Ben didn't see each other anywhere.

A year later, Cybill saw him at the supermarket, wearing his old maroon hoodie, but Lucy was by his side, and Cybill ducked into the spice aisle to avoid them. Anyway, she needed some Aleppo pepper.

14. PSYCHONAUT

2019

Years after she stopped having affairs—that is, several years after her beautiful mornings with Ben—Cybill still thought like an adulterer. When she met a girlfriend to go to a concert or reading, she always brought home the program, proof (not that any was needed) that she had indeed attended the event and not spent the time in some man's apartment. She still assessed the sexual potential of most men she encountered. When she sallied out alone, she made sure she was wearing good underwear, just in case. You're an old woman now, she would tell herself as she scrabbled through her panty drawer, looking for the green ones, you're over all that. And don't forget you have a very happy relationship. But it did no good to lecture herself: her body was faithful but her heart was a rogue.

Affairs had never been about sex to Cybill; they had been a way to achieve a certain kind of emotional intensity that can only be reached through uncertainty. Except with Ben, she had always been, or pretended to be, the underdog, the one who loved the most. It was important that her lovers keep her off balance. Then she could obsess about them and agonize about when she might see them again. But for some time now, this turbulence had seemed frivolous and irrelevant, and she was amazed that she had spent so much of her emotional life in thrall to one man or another.

Well, to be altogether honest, sex *had* been part of the appeal. Sexual novelty seemed to sharpen physical sensation, and she knew that without orgasm she wasn't likely to reach the emotionally abject state she craved. (Though what about Jasper?)

Just as criminals age out of being dangerous to society, so Cybill had aged out of sexual adventure. For most of her life, sex was always just around, part of the ambience, until one day it just wasn't. This coincided with a new prudishness in the culture, with flirtation taboo and unwanted touches a crime. Additionally, the candidates for adultery became sparse. Certainly, the men Cybill knew in her cohort were not very interesting. Worse, they were not very *interested*. The juice had gone out of these old guys: they didn't so much as raise an eyebrow or twitch a smile.

One afternoon, idly clicking and scrolling at her laptop, Cybill began looking at an appreciation of an avant-garde performance artist who had recently died at age eighty. She read the byline, Doug Kry, with a shock. It was such an odd name, it had to be him! She probably hadn't thought of him in decades, and, Cybill mused, if all the cells in your body are replaced every seven years, how was it possible that she still remembered him so vividly — or even at all? It was a mystery akin to the multi-generational migration of the monarch butterfly, Mexico-Canada and back.

She was going by ship to England for her junior year abroad. He was much older (twenty-six, she later learned), and he taught a poetry class every afternoon. He was articulate, witty, handsome, and remote: he met all her criteria. So she hung around after the second class and asked whether knowing how a poet treated his wife should affect what we think of his poems. "It's a complicated question," he replied. "Let me think about it." He gathered his books and stood up, ending their private chat.

Well, sure. An attractive and distinguished man like that (a Yale Younger Poet) must get mobbed by female students. Male ones, too. Actually, who knew if Kry even liked women? Homosexuality was Cybill's fallback explanation when a man she approached didn't respond. She went to her cabin and moped, writing about Kry in her journal until dinner.

✿ ✿ ✿

So when at the age of seventy-two, Cybill saw the name Doug Kry, it all came back to her: the student ship, the poetry class, and Yvon, whom she met the morning after Kry spurned her. Now, with arthritic fingers (bumps on her knuckles, numbness in her thumbs), Cybill went to DougKry.com. What would he look like now? The screen blinked to his page — and Cybill's heart lurched. There he *was*, the man she remembered, incredibly, scarcely changed! He had published many books of poems and taught at several colleges upstate. He also hosted poets and artists and had links to these events on his website. He was married, but she couldn't tell if he had children. She wrote to him on impulse.

Hello Doug,

I saw your fond tribute to Lyzette . . . and wow, your distinctive name! I was propelled back in time.

I went by boat to London for my junior year abroad, and on this boat you taught a poetry class. I probably had a crush on you--distinguished older man, maybe six years my elder.

Don't worry, this isn't #MeToo! You scarcely glanced at me and didn't break my heart! I soon met a Frenchman . . . I was constantly falling in love at the time, and I'm nostalgic now for this flighty intensity.

It's good to know you've had a life of poetry and art. Seeing your name was wonderful.

Cybill

What a flirt she still was. She thought: the young have no idea how mischievous the old can be.

He wrote back within the hour.

My my, Cybill, this sets a record for an email out of the blue referencing earlier times. Fifty-three years!

Yep, that was me, and it was my way of getting a free passage to Europe as some sort of floating instructor.

You should have gotten to know me then. I loved those between-reality voyages (I did four of them roundtrip, so eight passages) and the pleasure of being neither here nor there. I still love that feeling but now, though I do travel in the usual way, I do it mostly in the mind through writing and art as a "psychonautic." (They just yesterday decriminalized magic mushrooms in Denver!)

Your website is lovely and your history of work impressive—I watched your bio/video.

I imagine your life is even more fun. There are some videos on my own website.

Thanks for responding to my tribute to Lyzette, one of my oldest friends and a great artist, as I'm sure you know.

So, we should meet sometime and have a conversation belatedly. I'm up in the Hudson Valley near Rhinebeck.

With thanks for being in touch and warm wishes,

Doug

Fire. Cliché be damned! There was no other way to describe what went through her veins as she read his words. That he had written back so fast was just another cause for conflagration! And he wanted them to meet. He had seen her little video and wanted to see her in person. She reread the words "You should have gotten to know me then." Should she tell him she had tried? And when should she reply? She had to wait until at least tomorrow.

She needed the dictionary of slang to tell her that a psychonaut is someone who explores altered states of consciousness, especially through hallucinatory drugs. Maybe having lovers was how she had altered her consciousness. She put both her hands over her heart, which seemed to be rising and swelling, along with the rest of her.

So here she was again, elevated and electrified, abrim. To think that she had ever disparaged this state of affairs! This thrill, this urgency, this keen anticipation. This is me, Cybill thought, myself as crazy as ever! Molten. She managed to get dinner on the table and have a nice conversation with Quinn, but her mind was going Doug, Doug, Doug. Wiping the counter, glowing from within, Cybill thought surely this ecstasy was her truest, most essential self. How could she have forgotten?

That night, with one leg wrapped around Quinn, she kept waking from dreams about Doug.

She had been, in her wanton years, careful about her affairs. Except with Ben, she had rarely risked having a lover in her house: she would go to theirs or meet the man in a motel. Her motivation had always been wanting more, rather than compensating for less. She felt she just wasn't monogamous by nature, although she liked living with a man. So she had gone to great lengths not to imperil her relationship with Quinn. This did not include avoiding other men. It just meant she was prudent. What was odd was how this prudence still shaped her life many years after its necessity.

You see, I really did go to that concert, I really was at that restaurant with Johanna, and there is no one hiding in the guest room! Look, the door is wide open,

With Doug Kry wanting to see her, once again Cybill was consumed. When, when, when would they meet? And would it be near a hotel? Now she was giddy, insane, lost in solipsistic obsession. But she would try to keep it casual.

Hi Doug,

What fun to hear from you! I'm delighted you looked at my little video.

Yes, we should meet sometime. We can talk about our shared past (ha ha) . . . and much more about our unshared lives. Perhaps you'll let me know before your next trip to New York City and we can meet there.

I occasionally visit a friend in Kingston, which isn't far from you.

To art! And nostalgia! And email!

She did not expect to hear from him that afternoon. She had waited a day to reply to his first email, by which, she thought, she had implied they shouldn't rush things. But the day after that, she checked her email every hour, each time telling herself it didn't really matter. Hour after hour there was nothing from Doug. When three days passed without his writing back, she reread his sole email. Perhaps she was expected to look at the videos on his website. As was her habit, she had been in such a fever she had almost forgotten the actual person who had caused the inflammation.

She clicked on the most recent video link, the one entitled April 13, 2019. A pale old man began reading a difficult poem. He had a small tremor in the hand that held the paper. She wondered who the poet was and when Doug would appear on camera to speak about him. Then, with a shock, Cybill realized the poet was Kry. You could tell by the slant of his cheekbones and the shape of his mouth. But he was old! And why was she astonished? Wikipedia had revealed that he was 78. It was just that the man on the video looked so much older than the man on the website home page—like his father, or even his grandfather. Cybill fell back to earth, bumping along the ground.

Why hadn't he updated his website photo? Then she wouldn't

be in this thing in the first place. Not that she was in it any more, she reflected in the days ahead, so it didn't matter that he wasn't writing back. Or perhaps it was up to her to write (although technically it was his turn), to show that she accepted him as he was now. Or she could write to him out of gratitude that he had brought efflorescence to her life again, if only temporarily.

But she couldn't obsess about this man. Nor was anyone likely to obsess about her. They were elderly. He had reentered her life through a memorial piece. Their friends were dying. Perhaps he could no longer drive. By directing her to his videos, he was showing her who he was at present. He had written "You should have gotten to know me then" because it was much too late for them now.

And Cybill saw that while the habit of adultery would stick to her forever, from now on, her erotic adventures would be exclusively what they had largely been anyway. . . what was Kry's word?

Cybill smiled.

Psychonautic.

15. PASSION IN THE PANDEMIC

2020

When the virus hit New York and its suburbs, Cybill became newly aware of the gulf between her age and Quinn's. She was far more likely to get infected than he, and if she got it, she would suffer more. Indeed, she might die. People in their seventies crowded the obituaries, cause of death: "complications of the novel coronavirus." She wished they would stop calling it the *novel* coronavirus, for she had always had pleasant associations with the word "novel," in both of its meanings. And now the virus was mowing down the city. Two of her friends had caught it and were recovering slowly; a distant friend had died.

Every day the toll grew larger, hitting different groups: health workers, people in nursing homes, workers in warehouses—and always the old. She couldn't read the *New York Times* without tears.

After the state went into lockdown Cybill did a massive shop during an early-morning senior hour, after which she and Quinn practiced social isolation together; his school was closed. Day to day, life wasn't that different from before Quinn took his teaching job: he and Cybill were often alone in the house, sharing it easily, in their own worlds, often apart until dinner. But before the pandemic, there was always something to look forward to: a night out or a meal with friends or a visit from her kids or one of his band gigs. Now there were no gigs, weekdays and weekends were no different from each other, and there was no end in sight.

Cybill and Quinn had sex no more and no less than before, although they cuddled even more than usual and hugged when they passed each other during the day. She supposed they were both creatures of habit, each usually eating the same thing for breakfast and lunch five days a week (but not the same meals as each other), and at the same times (although not the same times as each other). She was glad she was past having affairs, and she pitied all the illicit lovers who couldn't get together during lockdown. Would the separation fan the flames higher or would it extinguish them? She supposed it was different in every case. Her affairs, she had come to believe, had been more about her mental disorientation than her physical satisfaction, so in her case, the separation would probably have intensified her passion.

Sometimes Cybill wondered why polyamory felt so natural to her, beyond her mother's lifelong bond with the Italian. Was it because as a child she'd been adored by two uncles, dandled on their knees, thrown into the air above their grinning faces? Surely other girls had had similar experiences and had grown up happy with just one man. How could you know what constituted a good explanation? Scientists said one test was if you could predict the future from it, but this was not possible with her uncle hypothesis.

Phone calls took up part of Cybill's pandemic days. She suddenly needed to have long, searching conversations with all of her friends. As much as she could, she used Facetime; she loved seeing people's faces and cherished their expressions. If she couldn't see them in person, at least she could see them here. One friend refused to use Facetime, saying she didn't want to be reminded of how old she looked. Everyone was getting frowsier; some had gained the "Covid-15." Quinn was growing a beard, which did not suit him. Johanna's hair was past her shoulders and getting bushy.

And everyone was suddenly Zooming. After her first Zoom call, when her image dismayed her, Cybill angled her webcam just right. She carefully positioned a lamp with a golden shade so the light worked like a bronzer. The face that looked back at her from the grid might as well have been an avatar, it was so idealized. You couldn't see the wrinkles and the shadows in such a small display. She was perfect for Zoom.

❈ ❈ ❈

Almost a year to the day after she'd had her brief and euphoric email exchange with Doug Kry, she opened her email to discover that Academia.edu had sent her an academic paper by him. She had never before received a document from the organization, and when she considered the tens of thousands of academic papers published all year, it seemed quite a coincidence that she had received his. Was it chance or did he want her to read it? Either way, her heart was racing. It slowed when she read the paper, some aspect of poetics which she found unfathomable. Despite what McHugh thought, it really was for the best that an academic career hadn't been hers. She emailed Doug:

> This morning Academia.edu, whatever that is, sent me something you wrote. This is the first time they have sent me anything, so it seems quite a coincidence that of all the academic papers published annually they sent me one by someone I know. Perhaps you asked them to send it to me— but why? Its content was mysterious to me! I hope you are well and stay safe.

These days, everyone was always hoping people were well and staying safe.

As had happened the year before, his reply to her initial email came instantly:

> Cybill —
>
> No, I had nothing to do with it, their algorithms make these decisions.
>
> You say I'm someone you know, well, we met over half a century ago and merely exchanged a couple of emails. So how did they link us? Do they have access to our address books?

She replied:

> You are not in my contacts or address book, so it is indeed
> creepy that on the basis of a couple of emails academia.edu
> notifies me of your upload.

She paused. Was that word "loaded"? Would he see it as
sexual? Whatever. Then, smiling as she typed, she continued,
because, after all, what did she have to lose?

> I never said I knew you well, but at this point I'm starting to think
> it is fated. We could divert each other during the pandemic.

She thought "divert" was the perfect word, suggestive but not
threatening. She had quite forgotten her conviction of the year
before that they were both too old for this sort of thing.

He replied the next day as if she hadn't used the word "divert."

> Academia connected me with another person, this one a dear
> friend from long ago, and we had a long talk today. Curious
> and enchanting. This has never happened before, and now
> twice.
>
> I must run now — more at another point.

"More at another point"! It seemed like a promise, so she
waited. She wondered if the close friend of years past was a
woman.

After a few days she wrote to him again, getting to know him
during the pandemic as they glided toward . . . what? What
exactly did she have in mind with this flirtation? Suggestive
emails, certainly; she looked forward to both receiving and
composing them. In the past, she had put some of her best

writing energy into emails to lovers, and she was sure she could summon it again. . . After the emails, then what? Surely, they would want to hear each other's voices, so phone calls would be next. Presumably, they'd soon advance to video chat. On seeing each other's faces in real time, would their flirtation blossom or break down? She wrote:

What are your plans on this beautiful day?

For it was finally sunny and warm. She thought: The big advantage of the e-affair was that you never had to feel guilty. It was all stimulation, no satisfaction, and for that, perhaps, all the more intense. She had it all worked out.

Only Cybill never heard from Doug Kry again. It took a while, but she finally had to acknowledge that he *really* wasn't interested in her. Hadn't been when she was twenty, nor last year, nor now. You had to be attracted to someone to want what she was proposing: nuanced and prolonged titillation. Doug's "More at another point" worked out to be "no point" and "goodbye."

This time, it took a mere ten days for her to stop expecting email from him, ten days for her inbox to become neutral again and not a place of hurt and disappointment. So much for her idea of their being fated!

Two months into lockdown, it occurred to Cybill that Doug Kry wasn't the only one who might divert her. Perhaps a past lover would suit. Some were so far in her past they would seem new to her again; others would surely display new aspects of themselves in an e-sex affair.

She remembered her rogue lover, Mel, with whom she'd had telephone sex. Telephone sex was still possible during a quarantine. She had last seen Mel at the Bliss workshop—what, almost twenty years ago? She smiled to recall his interest in Quinn. She wondered what Mel was up to now, where he was living, whether he was healthy. She sent an email to him, but it bounced back. She put his name into a Google search box . . .

and, to her sorrow, found a link to his obituary. Mel had been dead for four years, after working for a pharmaceutical company in Boston. It did not give a cause of death. Cybill hoped he'd died suddenly, in pleasure, perhaps while shaving a woman's armpit.

Dinners had become more elaborate now that Cybill had few other duties or activities. Since she couldn't dash out to get fresh mint or tamarind paste, she used plenty of substitutions when following recipes. Everything came out pretty well anyway, and almost everything required lemon zest. Now she always had naked lemons in her fruit drawer.

As she denuded yet another lemon for a pasta dish, Cybill contemplated contacting Jasper for a virtual affair. It would be good to see his handsome face again, onscreen, of course. He'd always been fun to talk to; they could continue those intense discussions, only not in person. She could not remember his voice, but she did remember his brown eyes and his hard hands. Soon, she remembered other things about him: his stiff and formal emails; his extreme caution. This was not a man who liked to play and flirt. And this was not a man who would embark on an affair, even a virtual one, in a house shared by a couple. He'd always been terrified of being discovered, of breaking up her marriage, although she wasn't married. No, Jasper wasn't the right man. To say nothing of how disappointing he'd been in bed! If a couple didn't have the present, and the future was unknown, they should at least be able to remember great sex in the past.

Then there was Ben. But Lucy would always be the barrier, the threat.

She and Quinn invariably watched TV after dinner. She was proud that they didn't watch during the day, except for the news and the Cuomo briefing at 11:30 in the morning. A decade younger than Cybill, Cuomo was something of a father figure to her: reasonable, responsible, reassuring. After dinner, there was a torrent of content to choose from on television, but somehow very little was compelling or memorable.

Cybill and Quinn had a special way of watching TV: he or she would lie on their back the length of the couch and the other, also on their back, would lie atop, with a pillow or two beneath head and neck. The person on top often kneaded the other one's feet, while the person on the bottom gave the other one a head massage. They were thus entangled when the telephone rang. Cybill was on top, so she got up to answer the phone.

"Cybill, this is Grania, Johanna's sister."

Fear crawled into Cybill's chest. "Hi."

"I'm afraid I have some bad news. Johanna died last night in the emergency room."

"NO!" Cybill put down the phone and pounded the telephone table with both fists. "No, no, no!" Then she picked up the phone again. "What happened? Was it the virus?"

"They don't know yet. She'll be tested. She called me with a terrible pain in her stomach, so I got my car and took her to the ER. As soon as we got inside, she had a heart attack and just ... died."

"But Johanna was always so healthy. She had no history of heart problems."

"I know. That's why I think it was Covid."

"I am so, so, sorry. I can't tell you . . . I can't believe it."

"These are terrible times," said Grania.

After Cybill hung up, she let herself wail and weep.

Quinn walked toward her with his arms open.

"Johanna died," she told him. "She just *died*."

"Oh, Cybill, no." He put his arms around her and patted her back.

She said, while gulping through tears, "She was so important to me. God, oh, God!"

Quinn kept patting her back until she impatiently threw off his hand and broke away from him.. "Johanna is *dead*. I will never ever see her again."

"I know, Cybill. I'm only trying to help."

"I know. It's just so sudden."

"She was what, seventy-four? People die at that age."

"Well, they don't just die. They die of a cause."

"It was probably the virus," Quinn said.

Cybill hoped he was right. It would be easier to mourn her death if it was part of a larger tragedy. It's one thing to lose your best friend; it's another to lose her to the pandemic. Either way: no Johanna to swill her glass of white wine and make a dire prognostication. No Johanna to shake her head so that her precisely-cut hair flared out. No Johanna to recommend a book or mock a celebrity or visit with some specialty bar of chocolate. How could that be? Cybill shook her head and shouted, "NO." She threw herself headfirst into the couch.

Quinn said, "I'll get you some tissues."

Cybill sobbed. "Nothing, and I mean *nothing*, is more important than people."

"It's true."

"This virus is killing so many *people*." She started crying again. "But Johanna! I always had her voice in my head, I always knew what she would say. Sometimes I defined myself against that voice, but it was still important. Oh, Quinn, what if I'm next?"

"You won't be next," said Quinn. "You have me to look after you."

Now her first thought every morning was No Johanna. Johanna is gone. When a good friend dies, Cybill thought, you not only lose the person, you lose the special entity you were together, your particular rituals, your jokes, your dynamic. It was impossible to believe that Johanna would never scold Cybill nor laugh with her again. All her talents, calligraphy, crocheting, fluent Spanish — gone. No Johanna. Not ever again.

The coronavirus test came back negative; Johanna would have died anyway. So Cybill couldn't claim a public sorrow; her mourning was more private. Still, she posted a few words about Johanna's death on FaceBook.

She got a condolence email from Lucas, of all people. Lucas and Cybill had stopped playing long distance Scrabble many years earlier, when she began seeing Jasper. Still, she continued to enjoy Lucas's Facebook posts, which were whimsical and full of puns. Now, she supposed, as someone with a chronic heart condition,

Lucas would do badly if he caught the virus. He wrote:

hi cybill,

i'm so sorry to hear about johanna. i met her a couple of times
when she administered an environmental grant i received.
she was a dynamic and witty woman. i didn't know her well--
not as well as u from the photos you've posted. i really liked
her, though. she was so smart, both ways—intelligent and
elegant. there was an undercurrent of sadness to her I always
wondered about. do u agree? it's terrible to think she's gone.
was it covid? how are u doing otherwise? have u managed
to stay saucy?

Cybill smiled for the first time in a week.

Hi Lucas,

It's good to hear from you on this very sad occasion. Johanna
and I met in college and became best friends at once, so it's
been devastating to lose her. No, not the virus, she tested
negative, she had a heart attack. I'd just spoken to her the
day before. I know what you mean about that inner sadness
of hers but she was so much fun anyway. As for me, I am not
very saucy right now. I am too sad.

Later that day he wrote:

maybe i can cheer u up

But she didn't see how. Was Lucas going to replace her best
friend? Suggest a way to find another? The idea of a virtual
affair now seemed preposterous: how could she have wanted
such an odd thing? Or sex at all, really. For the first time since
she'd gotten together with Quinn, she had no desire for him at

all. Still, the next time he put his hand on her breast, she let him. It was, after all, at their scheduled time, and it seemed easier to go along than to explain. But before they went much further, Quinn abruptly sat up, saying, "Another time."

"I'm sorry."

"You're grieving," he said. "I understand."

"You're such a fine man."

"Now what shall we have for breakfast?"

Downstairs, he read the paper while she cooked them omelets. He looked up to ask, "Hey, what's your blood type?"

"The top of the class," she said. "A+. Easy to remember. Why do you ask?"

"Oh, nothing. Mine's O+. I can give to you but you can't give to me."

"I hope that's not symbolic," said Cybill.

"You give me everything," he said, on cue.

She folded his omelet, cooked it 15 seconds more, and brought it to the table. Then she cooked her own.

After breakfast, she read the article that had prompted Quinn's question. She learned that people with type A blood were 50% likelier than others to get very sick if infected with the novel coronavirus. Her chances of dying had just gotten much greater. Death had come for Johanna and it might come for her.

She reviewed her will. She put her important papers into large file folder and told Quinn where it was. If she died now, she would never be a grandmother.

With the sense that death was moving in on her, she found herself interested in sex again, and on their next scheduled day, she touched Quinn's thigh before he reached for hers. It went very well. If I'm going to die, she thought afterwards, let me squeeze all I can from the time that remains.

Rage, rage against the dying of the light.

And then she heard from Lucas again.

how are you doing these days? feeling any better? i know the skies are gray but maybe you are warming up inside?

Lucas. She smiled. She wondered if he still wore his long wool coat and his long wool scarf.

She wrote back, and they continued to correspond. His emails cheered her up. His personal health had torn them apart, and now the public health, in the form of the pandemic, was bringing them together. They couldn't see each other in the flesh, but little by little, and day by day, they were getting close again. They even began playing Scrabble. So it wasn't a complete shock when he wrote

> i think we should move this party over to facetime. i want to look at you.

She agreed.

He hadn't changed much. He still had his hair, though it was grayer. He seemed to be sitting in a sun room. She was by the lamp with the gold shade.

"You've scarcely changed," he remarked.

"Flatterer."

"It's true. You're amazing."

"It's all lighting."

"And your breastworks?"

She laughed. "They're still here."

"Can I see?"

"No! Quinn's in the next room. What if he should come in and see me on the phone with my blouse open and my bra hiked up around my neck?"

"Yes!" cried Lucas. "Tell me more!"

So she did, closing the door and whispering about what she was not going to do. She told him she was not going to remove her shirt and bra and cup her naked breasts with her hands. And she was not going to show him her panties, nor take them off.

"You are such a vixen," he said happily.

"Gotta go now," she said and hung up.

She hoped that she had stirred him up a little. At this point, she herself was more entertained than titillated, but it was just the beginning. Or the rebeginning.

It was raining lightly. After a winter with almost no snow they were having a spring with almost no sun. And they were in the middle of a pandemic. Another distant friend had died, a handsome record producer her exact age.

Quinn tiptoed inside the house and motioned her to follow him outside. There, on the back lawn, was a doe and her fawn. Cybill had never been so close to a deer, let alone a fawn, and for several seconds everybody froze. Then the two deer ambled off.

"Wow," said Cybill.

"It's because of the pause," said Quinn. "There's so little traffic wildlife is returning."

"What a treat to see that fawn!"

Quinn held her close. He said, "I saw a fox on my morning run." For a while, they just swayed together in the rain.

When Lucas next called, she declined his request for video. "What's the matter?" he asked. "Still in your pajamas?" It was eleven o'clock; he knew her so little, she'd been up and dressed for hours.

"No, I just want to pull back some."

"Why do we have to do that?"

"We don't have to. But you'll enjoy it." She could hear Quinn strumming his guitar downstairs. She wondered where Maureen was, relative to Lucas.

He said, "What exactly will I enjoy?"

"I'm going to tell you a story and you're going to help me."

"A story!" said Lucas. "Boccaccio's young aristocrats told each other stories while escaping from the plague."

"This is our escape," Cybill said. "Once upon a time there was a pandemic, and two old lovers, in both senses of the word 'old,' slipped into a virtual affair."

"I see what you mean," said Lucas. "I'm already enjoying the story."

Cybill said, "Though they couldn't see each other in the flesh, they could evoke each other and provoke each other through their devices."

"Evoke, provoke, cute," he said. Then: "Hold on. I'm going to get more comfortable." After a few moments he said, "Go on."

"What did you just do?"

"Go on with your story," he said.

"So one day, they were talking on the phone, and he said 'Hold on. I'm going to get more comfortable.'"

"This is getting very meta," said Lucas. "You're telling a story about us even as it's unfolding in real time and in real life!"

"What's wrong with that? We tell stories to ourselves all the time, don't you think?"

"I guess."

"So then," Cybill continued, "she decided to spice things up a little."

"How did she do that?"

"You tell me," said Cybill.

Lucas said, "She decided to ask a pretty neighbor to join them."

Whoa! This was not what Cybill had anticipated and not the kind of threesome she had ever fantasized about: she liked the idea of two men. But there had to be give and take in a relationship, and she could be generous. "Well," Cybill said. "It wasn't her idea, but it meant a lot to him, so she invited Talia to come over."

Talia was wholly invented because her actual neighbors were not candidates for fantasy.

"Tell me about Talia," he said.

She described a young woman in great detail. Then she said, "You're in the middle between us."

"I'm in my happy place," said Lucas. She didn't have to say anything more.

The next time he called, he wanted Facetime, and she was ready for him in a loose cotton dress. She took the phone to the flattering nook she'd created. She had recently replaced the 75-watt bulb with a 40-watt bulb in the lamp with the golden shade, in case he wanted a look at her body.

Surprise! After a few minutes of banter, he did want to look at her body. She propped the phone on a shelf and lifted her dress. She counted, "One Mississippi, two Mississippi, three Mississippi." Then she let the dress fall again.

Lucas said, "No fair! You still have on your bra and panties."

Indeed she did, and her best ones at that.

"You've had your show," she said. "Now use your imagination."

"And memory," he said. "Don't forget how we did it."

"I don't," she said. "That's why we're here."

"But why are we here, Cybill? And where are we, really?"

She was silent, searching for something witty to say.

Lucas said, "I really want to know where we are."

This was a surprise. He was always so insouciant.

She replied, "Well, darling, for one thing, we're each in our own homes. We're happy with our partners, but we want a little more. Maybe we enjoy a little danger. And Johanna died. We could each die, too, from the virus — or anything else. So now, before it's all over, we're reaching for some intensity, some communion, some ecstasy, if only through our screens."

He said nothing.

"What do you think, Lucas? Is that about right?"

CPSIA information can be obtained
at www.ICGtesting.com
Printed in the USA
JSHW041442040223
37167JS00005B/23